Christie &Company

In the Year of the Dragon

Christie &Company

In the Year of the Dragon

KATHERINE HALL PAGE

AVON BOOKS  NEW YORK

This is a work of fiction. Names, characters, places,
and incidents either are the product of the author's
imagination or are used fictitiously. Any resemblance
to actual events, locales, organizations, or persons,
living or dead, is entirely coincidental and beyond
the intent of either the author or the publisher.

AVON BOOKS
A division of
The Hearst Corporation
1350 Avenue of the Americas
New York, New York 10019

Copyright © 1997 by Katherine Hall Page
Map by Virginia Norey
Interior design by Kellan Peck
Visit our website at **http://AvonBooks.com**
ISBN: 0-380-97397-9

Library of Congress Cataloging in Publication Data:

Page, Katherine Hall.
    Christie & Company in the year of the dragon / Katherine Hall Page.—1st ed.
        p.   cm.
Summary: Three roommates and amateur sleuths try to deal with a Chinese
    gang that is threatening the family of a friend.
[1. Mystery and detective stories.   2. Chinese Americans—Fiction.
    3. Gangs—Fiction.]   I. Title.   II. Title: Christie and Company in the year
    of the dragon.
PZ7.P142Ch1   1997   97-441
[Fic]—DC21   CIP

First Avon Books Printing: November 1997

AVON TRADEMARK REG. U.S. PAT. OFF. AND IN OTHER COUNTRIES, MARCA REGISTRADA,
HECHO EN U.S.A.

Printed in the U.S.A.

FIRST EDITION

QPM   10   9   8   7   6   5   4   3   2   1

To the Scovel Family—
Carl, Faith, Helen, Chris, and Rebecca—
for the blessings of their friendship
since I was Christie & Company's age

Acknowledgments

I had wonderful help on this book—and great fun, along with some memorable meals. I'd like to especially thank Kathy and Jasmine Chang; Kathleen Schaefer; Shuguang and Niklas Zhang; and Rebecca Scovel and the following students at the Atlantic Middle School in Quincy, Massachusetts: Emily Lam, Mabel Chan, Vikki Ho, Vera Lau, and Hoi Yee So.

As always, I'm grateful to have had the pleasure of working with Gwen Montgomery, my editor, and Faith Hamlin, my agent—and a long overdue thank you to my copyeditor, Carol Edwards.

Special thanks to my husband, Alan, and son, Nicholas, who make every year the Year of the Dragon for me.

"It's nothing, dear. Just something I saw quite suddenly which I ought to have seen before. . . ."

—Miss Jane Marple in Agatha Christie's
A Murder Is Announced

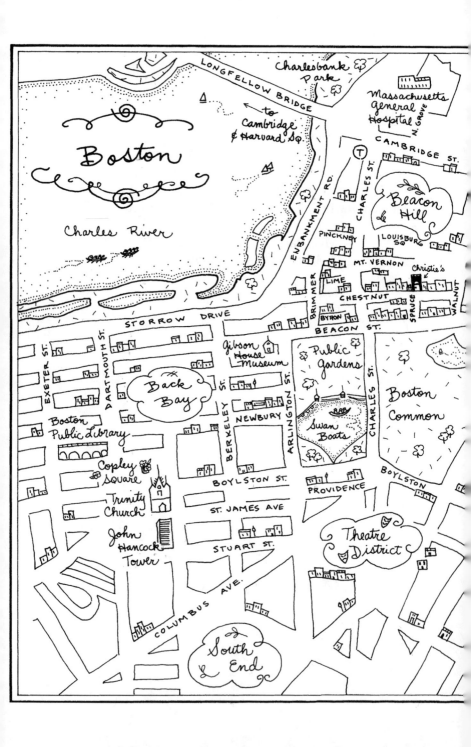

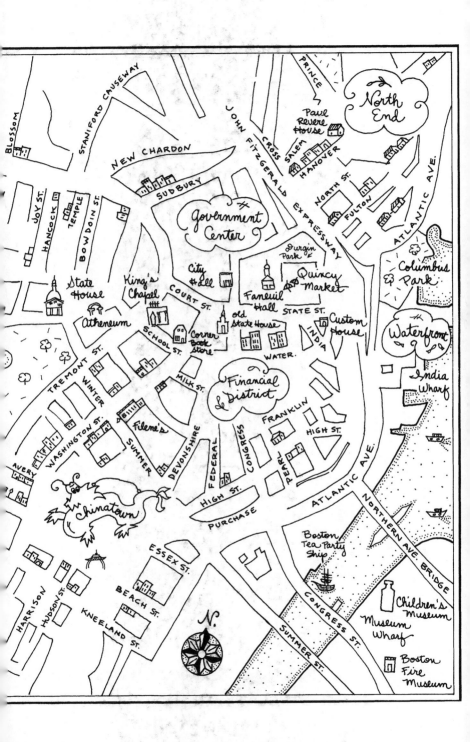

Chapter One

"Mrs. Babcox wants to see you in her office right away, Vicky," Ms. Stolfi, Vicky Lee's English teacher at the Cabot School, said, replacing the receiver of the intercom. "You'll have to finish the assignment on your own time and give it to me tomorrow."

Vicky gathered her things together, glad to avoid the boring grammar drill but puzzled—and vaguely apprehensive—about why Cabot's headmistress wanted to see her enough to pull her out of class. She left the white clapboard classroom building and crossed the campus, also white from a recent snowfall, to the main building. Cabot, located in Aleford, Massachusetts, about twenty minutes from Boston, was ninety-four years old, and the buildings definitely reflected each generation's idea of what a private New England boarding school should look like. This explained the variety of architectural styles, ranging from Prentiss House, Vicky's dorm—a Victorian gingerbread affectionately called "Widow" because of the useless, highly decorative widow's walk on top—to the sleek new glass sports complex. But, Vicky thought, looking about her, snow homogenized everything under one big milky-white blanket.

She scrupulously searched her conscience. She knew she hadn't done anything major—for example, been off campus without permission, especially in the company of one of the boys from Mansfield Hill Academy, conveniently situated in the same town. Not that it wouldn't have been fun—it just wasn't Vicky's style. The rules at Cabot were sensible and mostly about stuff you wouldn't do anyway. Had she unintentionally crossed some line? Done something and hadn't realized it was a no-no? She was sure she wasn't failing anything. In fact, she had been on honors since the first quarter, her very first quarter as a new girl.

She stopped short and gasped, covering her mouth with her hand. Mrs. Babcox must have eyes not just in the back of her head but all over her skull! How else could she have known that Vicky had ditched gym last week when the teacher was called away? A host of contradictory thoughts—explanations, recriminations—raced into her head. She hadn't cut *all* of gym. She'd been there for most of it, but she had slipped out after the teacher instructed them to "finish your sit-ups before showering." And really, Mrs. Babcox—Vicky was progressing to an imaginary conversation—you know I like gym and am going out for track and everything, but the hot water doesn't last long and I am a real chicken about cold showers and . . .

Another of Vicky's voices cut abruptly into her headlong ramblings. She knew it was wrong and could get her in trouble, but she'd done it anyway. And she had gotten caught.

By this time, she was at Mrs. Babcox's door. Vicky knocked, squared her shoulders, and prepared to face the music. The secretary called, "Come in," and Vicky tossed her long, straight black hair back over her turquoise parka and marched forward.

"Why don't you leave your things here?" the secretary suggested. Vicky was glad for the reprieve and left her heavy winter outer garments in a heap on a chair with her knapsack. Several pounds lighter, she knocked and pushed open the door to the inner sanctum.

"Come in, Vicky." Mrs. Babcox stood up and walked around her desk toward the eighth grader.

Deciding that honesty was the best policy, Vicky confessed, "I really did mean to finish the sit-ups another time. Except I have this problem with cold showers and . . ."

It was the headmistress's turn to look puzzled. "Sit-ups? I thought you were in English class, but no matter. I have a favor to ask you, a pleasant one, I hope."

Vicky was so relieved that it took a moment before she realized that Mrs. Babcox was gesturing toward the window. Someone was standing there regarding them both, someone who was now moving toward Vicky and speaking.

"*Ni hǎo má,*" she said.

"Fine. I mean, *wǒ hǎo.*" Vicky was so surprised, she

3

didn't know what language to use. The girl was Chinese!

"This is Blair Chan," Mrs. Babcox said. "She is joining the eighth grade, and although Blair's English is excellent, I thought it might help, especially in the beginning, if she had you to show her around, rather than one of the other girls."

"I'd love to," Vicky replied.

Unlike Vicky's hair, Blair's was cut short, a shining, silken cap that grazed her earlobes. Vicky was small and slight. Blair, about a head taller, had broad shoulders and, although not heavy, was solidly built. Her mouth had stretched into a wide smile at Vicky's words.

Vicky had meant what she said. This was going to be fun—possibly a new friend and a Chinese one at that! But now she had a million questions. Where was Blair from? Why was she entering Cabot in the middle of the year? Was she a boarder, like Vicky and her roommates, Maggie Porter and Christie Montgomery? Or a day student? And what about her name, Blair? It was common to change your Chinese name to an English one, but Blair was a pretty unusual name.

"Thank you so much," Blair said appreciatively. Vicky noted the relief in her eyes. The girl added, "I'm afraid I may end up needing a lot of help."

Which, as they discovered, was the understatement of the year—the Year of the Dragon.

"She had to leave right after that. She's a day student and will be commuting to Boston. I'm meeting her first thing in the morning at the bus stop. Our schedules are practically the same!" Vicky was sprawled out on her bed in the room she shared with Christie and Maggie. It was almost dinnertime.

"What else do you know about her? Why is she starting so late in the year?" Maggie wanted to be a writer, and she carried a pad and pencil in her pocket so she could jot down ideas or anything else that struck her. She went through a lot of notebooks. She also religiously wrote in her journal each night. "If you don't write every day, you're not really serious," she'd told her roommates. And Maggie was serious— but also a daydreamer. One part of her mind was already sketching out an elaborate plot, with Blair Chan as the main character.

"She told me she'd fill me in tomorrow—or rather, us," Vicky replied. "She can't wait to meet you. All I know is that she lives in Chinatown with her mother and little brother. He must be really little, because the reason she was in such a big rush was that she had to pick him up at day care. And she joked that she's sure to get lost a lot. Cabot seems like a big place to her." Which, Vicky reflected, it was when you compared it to the densely populated, crowded-together neighborhood of Boston's Chinatown. Cabot was spread out over forty acres, much of it woods.

"Do you speak the same dialect?" Christie was as interested in their new classmate as the others. From Vicky, she'd already learned a great deal about China. Vicky had been born in Hong Kong, but her parents were from mainland China. Vicky spoke both Mandarin and Cantonese.

"Blair was speaking Mandarin, but that doesn't really tell us anything about where she's from. It could be Taiwan, Hong Kong, or China—Mandarin is spoken in all three places, although if she had been born and raised in Hong Kong, I'd expect Cantonese to be her first language. I also noticed she had a Chinese quilted winter jacket. It was on the chair, so obviously she hasn't discovered Filene's Basement yet." Vicky was a clotheshorse, but a frugal one, and the discount store in downtown Boston was one of her favorite haunts.

"It could also mean she hasn't been here very long or comes from a very traditional family—or, heaven forbid, isn't as interested in what she wears as you," Christie added.

All three girls were avid mystery readers and adept at spotting clues. Maggie was wearing her deerstalker hat, a habit she'd picked up from Sherlock Holmes. She said it helped her concentrate, but she only sported it in the privacy of her own chambers. "Too geeky in public," she said. However, she did wear the mystery T-shirts from her growing collection. Christie had been in Washington, D.C. over the holidays and had found Maggie a great one: SO MANY MYSTERIES, SO LITTLE TIME.

"You said Blair mentioned her mother and brother. What about her father?" Maggie asked.

Vicky shook her head. "She didn't say anything about him. Maybe he's back in Taiwan, or wherever."

Or dead, Christie said to herself. She had lost her own mother to breast cancer almost a year ago, and she hoped Blair wasn't going through the same kind of thing. The pain was always with Christie, a dull ache—the constant realization that she would never see her mother again—or sometimes it was sharper, a feeling that made her dizzy and scared. During the fall, with Vicky and Maggie's encouragement, she'd started seeing someone at Cabot's counseling center, and it was helping. Still, her first thought was death, not absence or divorce. Maybe Blair wasn't very close to her father. Please, let it just be that, she said to herself.

Last month, Christmas, the first Christmas without Molly Montgomery, had been very hard. Christie's father, Cal Montgomery, a lawyer, had tried his best. They'd spent the actual day with Christie's mother's family in Connecticut, then taken off for New York City and Washington—lots of plays, museums, and interesting restaurants. Christie had been able to tell her father before the holidays how she felt. She didn't want them to duplicate the family rituals of the past. Sick as Mrs. Montgomery had been the Christmas before, she had struggled to maintain their traditions—sending Christie and her father to the *Nutcracker* ballet, making a gingerbread house with her daughter, and appearing at Christie's bedside Christmas morning, a frail figure carrying the tray they'd always used, which held Christie's laden stocking, cocoa, and cinnamon toast for the three of them. Maybe Christie would do these things with her own children, she told her dad, but for the foreseeable future, she wanted a holiday as unlike the old ones as possible. He had agreed and whirled them away.

Vicky and Maggie exchanged glances. They knew what Christie wasn't saying. The three had dubbed themselves Christie & Company while solving a particularly nasty crime at Cabot last fall in which they were the prime suspects. By now the girls could almost always tell what each other was thinking. Christie & Company.

Christie's parents had originally met on the subway in Boston. They had been sitting across from each other, reading the same Agatha Christie mystery. They named their daughter after that auspicious first meeting. The girl "detectives" adopted the famous mystery writer's name for themselves, too. Christie & Company—it was a good name.

"The class can use somebody new. You don't think she'll get all caught up with Marcia's precious little group, do you?" asked Maggie.

"I doubt it," Vicky said. "She seemed too . . . well, down-to-earth." Blair Chan had had a definite twinkle in her eyes when she had joked about the possibility of getting lost. Marcia Lloyd's clique didn't share Christie & Company's sense of humor. They were superintense about how they looked—the same—what class offices they held—all of them—and various members of the Mansfield Hill Academy student body—boys from the "right" families.

Vicky was also sure that a girl from Chinatown might encounter some of the subtle and not-so-subtle racism Vicky herself had. Her parents owned The Ginger Jar, a popular Chinese restaurant in Brookline, Massachusetts, and Vicky remembered the slighting remarks about the kind of meals where you got hungry again an hour later and the whispered imitations of what they thought were hysterically funny Chinese accents—and Blair's would make her an easy target. No, this new girl would not be adopted by Marcia Lloyd and her friends. She'd find a pleasant niche with the rest of the eighth grade, as Christie & Company had, especially with the twins, Imani and Aisha Brooks, boarders from Boston's South End, and Marine Collonges, a French student. These girls had volunteered to be Christie & Company's guides, an old Cabot tradition. She wasn't an old girl yet, but Vicky decided to ask her housemother if she could be Blair's Cabot Guide.

"We're going to be late for dinner," Christie said suddenly, jumping up from the comfortable, worn easy chair where she'd been trying to read her history assignment and listen to the others at the same time. "Plus, I'm starved!"

"You're always starved," Maggie teased. It was true, though. Christie was a competitive diver and the rigorous training gave her an enormous appetite. "I hope it's not something like lasagna tonight," Maggie continued, "something with gooey cheese." She was vigorously brushing her long, wavy reddish-brown—Maggie called it "mousy brown"—hair. Her braces reflected back at her from the mirror, flashing in the light. She clamped her mouth tight. Almost everybody else had finished with wires, rubber bands, and retainers. Maggie was just starting.

When she was nine, her parents had left Manhattan for the Blue Heron Inn on Little Bittern Island, off the coast of Maine. Owning and running an inn had had its ups and downs, but they all loved the island and their new life. One of the disadvantages had been that there hadn't been any practical way for Maggie to get to an orthodontist earlier. A ferry, the *Miss Hattie,* or your own boat was the only way on and off the island. In fact, Maggie had come to Cabot, her mother's alma mater, because taking the ferry to the mainland after Maggie had graduated from the island's elementary school had been exhausting. With the long holiday break, she'd seen more of her parents and younger brother, Willy, this year than at the same time last winter, when the weather had forced her to stay with friends so many stormy nights. But with Cabot had come braces, and she hated them.

"Mags, you have got to stop being so stupid about your braces!" Vicky gently pushed her friend toward the door. They *would* be late to dinner, and it was embarrassing to arrive last, after everyone else had started. "You're going to look gorgeous, and tons of kids have them. You only notice *yours*. Besides," she added, giggling, "it's not as if you have a boyfriend." They all laughed at that as they walked through the cold late-January air to the dining hall. A Cabot girl and Mansfield boy had become literally entwined during the last dance the two schools had together and one of the chaperones had had to get wire cutters to set them free.

"I'll probably have them until I'm thirty or something and end up an old maid making beds at the inn all my life and fighting with Mom." These were two of Maggie's main pastimes at the Blue Heron— at least in her mind.

"Come on, let's run," Christie called, jogging ahead. "I'm not just hungry; I'm freezing."

The other two raced to catch up, their breath sending puffs streaming into the cool air like old locomotives trying to get up over the next hill. The well-lighted path to the dining hall was lined with evergreens, their branches weighed down by the glistening snow. Maggie looked at the sky. The moon hadn't risen yet and the stars were bright.

As they raced across the steppes, the wolves were so close to the sleigh that she could see their large yellow eyes. Their piercing howls rose above the sound of the storm that had engulfed the travelers shortly after they left the dacha. The driver turned and screamed over the din, "I don't think we can make it! I can't see a foot in front of us!"

She looked down at the feverish child wrapped from head to toe in furs. "I'll drive. You hold the child. He will die if we don't get to the doctor in Saint Petersburg." She threw off her heavy sable-lined cape and climbed next to the driver, seizing the reins. She drove like one bewitched. He crossed himself. His mistress was truly not of this world. The sleigh flew faster and faster. . . .

"Maggie, come back to earth. We're here." Christie poked her roommate. She was used to Maggie's sudden flights of fancy. "Come on! Take your things off. You're in luck. It's beef stew. Nothing remotely resembling chewing gum."

As she hung up her coat, Vicky gave a thought to Blair Chan. Was this winter weather new to her? She hadn't been wearing boots, but heavy shoes—not Doc Martens, some kind of imitation. In any case, they offered little protection against the snow and slush.

Soon the girls joined a table of other eighth graders chattering away and began digging into their stew. The food at Cabot was plentiful and appetizing, but definitely not Chinese, Vicky noted, her thoughts drifting back to Blair again. Weekends home and care packages dropped off by her doting father kept Vicky from missing Cantonese cuisine too much. Blair, as a day student, would eat lunch with them. Maybe she preferred ham and cheese on rye to steamed dumplings. Some of Vicky's Chinese-American cousins did. Finding out was going to be very interesting.

They were finishing the warm fruit compote that was tonight's dessert when a girl dressed all in black, with a rainbow-colored silk scarf tied around her neck, walked over to their table and rested her empty tray at the end. One ear had no holes; the other had five, each sporting a tiny jewel. Her face looked very pale, even for the time of year, and contrasted sharply with her shoulder-length jet black hair. "Nice sonnet, Margaret," she said, bowing her head slightly in Maggie's direction before moving on. Staring after her, Maggie had not been able to utter a word.

"I've seen that girl before; obviously, you wouldn't forget her. Isn't she in tenth grade?" Christie commented.

"Yes, she's in tenth. We're in Mr. Ropeik's writing seminar together." Maggie had been over the moon when she got accepted into the select class.

"What's her name?" Vicky asked.

"Amber St. James," Maggie said, and the sigh that followed was audible.

Christie and Vicky looked at their roommate, then at each other.

"Uh-oh," mouthed Vicky.

Christie nodded.

🐉 Chapter Two

It was several days before the girls' curiosity about Blair Chan was satisfied. Vicky heard bits and pieces about Blair's life as she guided her through the intricacies of Cabot life. The schedule, the homework, even the weather, which continued to pile snow on the ground, were a bit overwhelming. While Blair remained cheerful, her constant refrain was, "Can't talk; must run!" And she *did* get lost, despite Vicky's best efforts.

Finally, Friday arrived, a half holiday for the students, bestowed every once in awhile by Mrs. Babcox when she thought her students might benefit from a little breathing space. The three roommates had promptly arranged to spend the weekend in Boston. Maggie would stay at Christie's, and Vicky would have a chance to visit her own family.

"My parents will be busy at the restaurant, but at least we'll see one another and I'll have some time with my grandmother. I feel a little guilty that I haven't been with her in awhile."

Mr. Lee's mother had come with them from Hong

Kong, and during those first years when her son and daughter-in-law were working long hours, seven days a week, establishing their business, she had taken care of Vicky. They had a special bond with each other, despite her gentle teasing of her outgoing granddaughter, her "little peacock"—so different from the young girls of Mrs. Lee's youth in China. But, she reminded herself, peacock feathers brought good luck.

Each time Vicky saw her now, old Mrs. Lee seemed to have faded slightly, and her granddaughter worried that one day she would simply vanish forever, like the photographic images in old daguerreotypes. There was nothing specifically wrong, just bones that threatened to snap when Vicky hugged her too hard and once round, glowing cheeks, now flat and pale. Vicky shook her head to chase the thought from her mind.

"Shouldn't Blair be here by now?" Maggie fretted. Vicky's older cousin Teddy, who was at Harvard and had a car, was coming to pick them up. Blair's mother had given her permission to drive in with the girls and eat at The Ginger Jar; then Teddy would take her home and drop the other two girls at Christie's. Teddy's girlfriend lived on Beacon Hill, not far from the Montgomerys, and Chinatown was close by.

Vicky jumped up to peer out the window. It was a bright sunny day and the snow had stopped. Girls were sledding and a few were on cross-county skis. "There she is!" Vicky opened the window and called out. The girls could barely hear Blair's reply, but the word *lost* was definitely part of it. They burst out laughing and left the door of room thirteen well ajar. Blair had been there before, yet, with her sense of direction, they weren't taking any chances.

Room thirteen was on the third—top—floor of Prentiss House and had been carved out of a much larger space. The window curved around a turret and had a window seat. Off to the side, there was a deep alcove, almost another room, with a closet and a bed. It had been the place Christie, the first arrival, chose last September. Her need for privacy was less now, but she still treasured her snug nook. The rest of the room was "Dorm Modern" with plain, sturdy furniture and off-white walls. The only other remnants of Widow's glorious past were two highly decorative, nonfunctional gas wall sconces and an elaborate plaster medallion in the middle of the ceiling with floral garlands that once must have encircled a chandelier. The ninth-grade dorm was a newer one, and all three girls, especially Maggie, were beginning to dread next year's move. Widow was their home!

"Sorry I'm late. I got—"

"We know—lost," Christie said. Now all four girls laughed. Blair took off her jacket and unwound several heavy scarves from her neck. Her dark eyes were bright, as was her face, and she was slightly out of breath from running.

"Don't worry," Vicky reassured her. "Teddy's always late. We could go into the common room and have some cocoa or tea while we wait."

Blair rubbed her hands together. "Tea would be wonderful."

Each floor had a common room with a sink, a small refrigerator, a hot plate, and an ironing board and iron. It was another tower room, larger than Christie & Company's.

Blair sank into the big overstuffed sofa. "I love it here—and this room is so pretty." She nodded approvingly at the green-and-white-striped wallpaper, muslin curtains, and framed prints on the walls. "It's so American."

"You mean so New England," Maggie said. "It would look pretty strange out in the Southwest or another part of the country, but I know what you mean. It's like the parlor from *Little Women* or some other book. All we need is Beth's piano and Marmee in a rocking chair doing her mending."

"And Jo coming in with ink on her face," Blair added. Seeing their quizzical looks, she said, "I read all those books—*Rebecca of Sunnybrook Farm, A Girl of the Limberlost, Anne of Green Gables*—but tell me, why were they all 'of' someplace and not 'from'?"

Maggie thought she ought to have an answer for this, but she didn't. "Maybe that's the way people said it in those days. I'd be *Maggie of Little Bittern*. I could ask Mr. Ropeik—he teaches this English seminar I'm taking," she explained for Blair's benefit.

Christie interrupted hastily. They'd been hearing more than enough about the seminar, and particularly Amber St. James, who, according to Maggie, would have put Shakespeare out of business had she been born a few centuries earlier. Privately, Vicky and Christie wished Amber *had* been born then, or even just enough years ago to be out of Cabot by now.

"How do you know about all these old books?" Christie asked. "I read them because they were my mother's and grandmother's favorites."

"So did I," Maggie said. "Where did you find them? Are they translated into Chinese?"

Not to be left out, Vicky mumbled that she had read some of them, too, and had seen the movies. She preferred more modern heroines.

Blair looked at their expectant faces. "This has been such a crazy week. We haven't had much time to talk, and I've been so happy to have friends like you. At my old school, I wasn't close to anyone. Maybe because I hoped I'd be coming here."

"How *did* you end up here?" From what Vicky had said about Blair and what Blair herself had said, Maggie was sure Blair's background was going to make an interesting story. She almost reached for her little notebook, but instead she added, "I don't mean to be nosy. It's just that I like to know people's stories—I mean their lives, who they are and where they came from."

"Yeah, she's not nosy at all—just tell her everything!" Vicky enjoyed needling Maggie, yet it was the question *she'd* been wanting to ask, too.

"English is such a funny language." Blair laughed. "I know what *nosy* means, but why not your ear? Wouldn't that make more sense? *Eary?* Wanting to hear? But I am happy to tell my story." She encircled her mug of hot tea with both hands and brought it close to her face. The steam curled up over her dark bangs. She seemed to be gathering her thoughts, and enjoying the slightly dramatic pause.

"My father's family was from Beijing—the capital of China. At first, they were happy, because it seemed that many of the worst things of the past would change and the terrible fighting that had been tearing the country apart would stop. That there would be equality among people, no more famines or sickness. You know how huge China was, and things had been very, very bad."

Vicky nodded. She knew all about this from her parents and grandmother. "China still is huge and still has the problems," she said. "Four million square miles and home to more than one point two billion people, which roughly means that one out of every five people on earth is Chinese!"

Maggie hadn't realized this. It was hard to imagine. She started to ask a question, but Christie was speaking. "Please, go on with your story." Blair drank some of her tea and continued.

"After a time, my father's family realized the political system had changed, except not necessarily for the better. Some decisions didn't make any sense at all. My grandfather was a science teacher and he was forced to work in the fields, to be 'reeducated.' He had never labored in the countryside, and so he became quite ill. My grandmother was very worried, and together they escaped to Taiwan. They never saw their parents or their country again.

"My father was born in Taiwan, but as he grew up,

he felt restless. He was not Taiwanese, yet he wasn't really Chinese, either, and he didn't want to return, even when things began to change again. He had always heard about the United States and he decided to come—but one problem. My father and mother had fallen in love and there was not enough money to pay for a passage for both of them. Also, she was younger and he did not want to take her away from her family when he didn't know what life here would be like. It was a *big* problem, and he decided to come here and then send for her when he was established, but my mother is very determined. Maybe she was afraid an American girl would steal him away!" Blair laughed, and the girls knew this was a family joke.

"They got married before he left." Maggie was so sure, she didn't even put it as a question.

"Right! As I said, my mother is very stubborn!"

"Tell me about it," Vicky said, and Maggie nodded emphatically. So far, the score in what Maggie privately referred to as the "Mom Wars" was Mom roughly 8 million and Maggie maybe 102. And Vicky often referred to her own Chinese mother as "the immovable object."

"It's a good trait," Blair said, digressing. "I hope I'll be the same."

"Only different," Maggie added, qualifying this. Sharing a trait with Mom was one thing. Being like her, entirely another.

"Anyway," Blair continued, "shortly before my father left, they were married, and soon she discovered that he had left her with what she calls 'her precious gift.' Me!"

Maggie stared into Blair's face, storing away every word. "That's beautiful," she said softly.

"I don't know how beautiful I am," Blair said, "but it made my mother very happy. Like having a part of my father with her, since it would be so many years before they could be reunited."

"How long was it?" Christie asked.

"Almost twelve years," Blair answered.

"Twelve years!" Maggie wondered how it would be not seeing your dad for that long. Blair wouldn't have even known him or he her.

"He worked very hard to save money to bring us here, except he also had to send money to his mother, who was a widow now, and other family members. It was his duty. And my mother had to take care of her parents. Finally, the passages and papers were arranged so we could join him."

Blair took another sip of her tea and remembered the long journey. Over eight thousand miles from Taiwan to New York, then another plane to Boston. She had often seen planes flying overhead, but to be in one hurtling through the sky on her way to a new country was the most exciting thing that had ever happened to her.

"My father was waiting for us at the airport at the end of our journey. We all cried, and he took us to our new apartment. It was wonderful. He was very happy because he was not working in a restaurant kitchen anymore, but in the restaurant's office. When he first came, he didn't speak any English, and he washed dishes; then eventually he got other jobs in restaurants and studied English whenever he could. My father was very ambitious, and keeping accounts was what he had studied in Taiwan."

Christie felt the back of her neck tighten. Blair had said "was."

The two girls looked at each other. "Like your mother, my father is also dead. Vicky told me."

Christie put her hand on Blair's shoulder. "I'm so sorry."

"He had accomplished what he meant to do. He brought us here and got us settled. My mother knew right away he was sick, only she did not tell me for a long time. She wanted me to treat him normally. You must think he was a stranger, but he wasn't. All those years he wrote to me, first in Chinese, then in English. He wanted me to learn English before I came. For both my parents, education has been the most important thing in the world! I went to classes in Taiwan after my regular school, and there was an American lady, Mrs. Blair Samuels, who heard about me and loaned me her books, all those "Girl of" books. I took her name when I came here. No one could pronounce my Chinese name, Bì Yún."

Blair stopped speaking for a moment. She remembered how embarrassed she had felt at the school in Boston whenever people tried to imitate the sound that was so natural to her—her name. She took the name of her friend out of respect for her and all she had done and because it was the only English name she knew remotely resembling Bì. She had assumed it was a common name, as common as Yīng, which means "pretty" for girls at home—or rather, her old home.

"Now I know what he was doing," she told her new friends solemnly. "My father was afraid my mother would be here in this country, unable to speak the language, with no one to take care of her. He passed his job to me."

"Doesn't your mother speak English?" Christie asked.

Blair shook her head. "Before we came here, she was always working so hard, and then when she got home, she had to take care of the meals and do everything for my grandparents. There was no time. When we first arrived, she started classes at the Chinese church, but soon my father was ill and couldn't work. She got a job sewing at home, so she could take care of him."

It was a familiar story to Vicky. She knew many Chinese-American kids her age who acted as translators for their parents. Even when the adults had lived here a long time, it was hard to learn English. Like the cultures, the languages were vastly different. Written Chinese wasn't based on an alphabet with sounds, like English was. Instead, characters started out about five thousand years ago as pictographs. She looked at the girls sitting around the table and thought of the character for the word *friend*—two hands working in the same direction. As time went by, the pictures became more stylized and the images less easy to recognize. In more recent times, 1979, the pinyin system was introduced so characters for names, places, and other things could be written using the English alphabet.

Words in Chinese are usually only one syllable long, but that syllable can be pronounced in four different ways, four "tones." One character tells how to pronounce the word; another character is added to indicate what it means. In pinyin, four symbols— ˘, ¯, `, and ´—tell how to say the word, your voice rising, falling, staying flat, or curving! Vicky had gone to Chinese school on Saturdays when she was younger to learn how to write Chinese and understand her traditions and history.

While Vicky was thinking about her heritage, Maggie was thinking about how many different worlds were all going on at the same time. When she'd been up in Little Bittern worrying about the fog and whether the ferry could get back home from school on the mainland, Blair was watching her father die.

It was almost as if Blair had read her mind. "My father had lived a good life. He had many friends here, and even though we were separated in miles, we were always in his thoughts. He worked hard to make things the way he wanted them for us, and he lived long enough to see his son born. It was a very happy time. He was content at the end. My mother was proud to be married to someone so honorable and kind."

The girls nodded solemnly and Vicky asked, "How old is your brother?"

"He's five months old, and so smart! He can sit up and wiggle around the floor, almost crawling. He talks all the time, too, only not in a language we recognize! I know he will be just like his father." Blair sounded like a proud mother as much as a sister.

"We still don't know how you ended up at Cabot," Christie pointed out. Blair's story was beginning to resemble the *Arabian Nights*. It could well take a thousand and one evenings to hear the whole thing.

But before Blair could start on this next chapter, Vicky jumped up and exclaimed, "I forgot all about Teddy! He must be here by now!" She ran to the window. "There's his car. He's probably downstairs. I'll clean up and you guys go grab your stuff from the room. Tell him I'll be right there."

"What does yours say?" Maggie asked. She had broken her fortune cookie and exchanged the slip of paper inside with Christie for good luck. Blair and Vicky were doing the same.

" 'Many memorable adventures are in store for you!' That's always good news. What about yours?" Christie asked.

"It's kind of weird. 'Be careful! Straight trees often have crooked roots.' " As she read it out loud, Maggie got a shivery feeling. She thought all fortune cookie predictions were supposed to be super-cheerful.

"I think it means sometimes people or things aren't what they appear to be. Don't be fooled, that's all," Vicky said.

Vicky nudged Christie under the table. Who said

fortune cookies didn't tell the truth? Maggie was certainly falling under Amber's spell and, Vicky thought to herself, it wasn't hard to spot the false roots. Amber's jet black hair was definitely light brown at the part!

Blair read hers out loud: " 'Good to begin well; better to end well.' " Vicky's parents had joined the girls while they ate, and now Mrs. Lee nodded approvingly. She and Blair had immediately started speaking Chinese and she'd taken the girl for a tour of the restaurant. It was clear that she approved of Blair very much. Vicky had noticed right away the look her mother gave to Blair's dark pants, crisp white blouse, and rose-colored cardigan, worn buttoned up; contrasting the outfit with her daughter's—baggy overalls, tightly belted with a wide striped tie from a thrift shop, worn over an Irish fisherman's sweater. Vicky had braided one section of her hair, letting the rest hang loose. She was happy with her appearance, but she knew instantly her mother wasn't. Her mother wasn't happy with the "Tommy Girl" she'd liberally sprayed on, either. Mrs. Lee had wrinkled her nose after greeting her daughter. Apparently, she preferred a whiff of plain old soap to Hilfiger's cologne.

"You haven't read yours, Vicky," Christie said. She had enjoyed the meal. Mr. Lee kept bringing more and more dishes out—egg drop soup, crispy anise-flavored duck, stuffed bean curd, mountains of steamed vegetables, to name a few—but now she was eager to get home. It had been several weeks.

" 'Try your best to avoid arguing with your elders and superiors.' Mom! You planted this one!" Vicky accused her, only half in jest.

Mrs. Lee raised her hands in protest. "Do you think I read all these? But you know what they say . . ."

"Fortune cookies don't lie. Okay, okay." Vicky wasn't sure why she was suddenly feeling so out of sorts, but she wished Teddy, who had driven to her family's apartment to get their grandmother, would get back. It wasn't that she wanted her friends to go, but she was very conscious of the comparisons her mother was making between her and Blair Chan. And even when Blair left, there wouldn't be anything Vicky could say to her mother that wouldn't make her sound like a spoiled brat.

At some point in the last few years, her relationship with her mother had changed completely. Vicky knew her mother loved her. It was just that anytime Vicky tried to talk to her or get close, even to hug her, her mother would find some excuse—and with a busy restaurant to help run, it wasn't hard. Vicky made resolution after resolution to force her mother to tell her what had made things change. What had Vicky done? Yet she was afraid—afraid her mother would brush her off, saying it was nothing, or afraid it *would* be something. Vicky tried talking to her cousin Teddy—he was like her older brother—but he had his own worries. He was very serious about a non-Chinese girl and his parents were having a hard time accepting Caitlin and the possibility that their adored, successful only son might marry her. Who would take care of them in their old age? they asked him. How would she understand their ways?

Christie and Maggie kept urging Vicky to speak with her mother, or maybe talk to her father first.

Vicky rubbed her forehead. She was so confused.

"Headache, little one?" It was her grandmother, and Vicky turned to the old woman joyfully, grabbing the hand that had lightly stroked her forehead. Then she stopped, stunned. Her mouth dropped open and words froze in her throat. What had happened to her grandmother!

The woman looked ten years younger!

🐉 Chapter Three

"You can let me out here. I don't want to take you out of your way," Blair said, gesturing to a subway stop.

"It's hardly out of the way at all," Teddy Lee assured her. "Besides, Mrs. Babcox would never let me escort you again if I didn't put you down safe and sound on your own doorstep. I like my job as semi-official Cabot chauffeur. My cousin's friends have provided me with constant stories to tell back at Winthrop House, and I'm sure you'll do the same."

"Teddy!" Maggie shrieked, "What are you saying about us!"

"Oh, nothing too terrible," he teased her. "I just let my fellow students know that if they need any detective work done, they should forget Spenser or Hercule Poirot and get Christie and Company instead!"

Blair looked confused. "Detectives? You are detectives?"

"I guess we have provided some stories," Christie answered. "We're not real detectives, of course, but we've read so many mysteries that our little gray cells are not bad at figuring things out."

Teddy glanced over his shoulder at Blair. She was a cute kid, yet very different from his little cousin, who had grown up here and often looked like a *'TEEN*—or *Vogue*—magazine clipping. Blair was definitely an FOB, "fresh off the boat," but give her another year or so and she'd be like Vicky and her friends—even if her parents weren't crazy about some of her new ways, and few parents were. He knew Vicky thought his aunt Virginia was too critical, and it was hard for his little cousin to understand how differently her mother had been raised. He hadn't given it much thought until he was in high school and one of his girlfriends had constantly complained how hard it was to convince her mother to let her use things like underarm deodorant—and shave her legs. In turn, her mother thought her daughter as well as American women were nuts. East meeting West was often like those school dances where all the guys hung out on one side of the gym and the girls on the other; then, right before it was time to go home, everybody started to have a good time. He laughed aloud at the image.

"What's so funny?" Maggie asked. She was still wondering what Teddy was saying to his friends about them.

"Just an image that popped into my head. I was thinking how different and strange everything must have seemed to Blair when she first came here—and probably still is."

Blair nodded emphatically. "The hardest part was last year at school. The teachers had such a funny accent, and the food at lunch!" She made a face that said it all.

"Are you near Washington Street? Because we're almost there. Tell me where to turn," Teddy said.

For a moment, Blair looked confused. Maggie was surprised. Surely she didn't get lost in her own neighborhood. What was going on?

"Left past the next light, then halfway down the block on the left, on Harrison," Blair blurted out rapidly. Teddy followed her instructions.

"Oh," he said, after she called out, "Here it is—you live at Tai Tung Village. You should have said so. I know it well." Tai Tung was an apartment complex not far from the center of Boston's Chinatown.

Blair thanked him, said good-bye, and jumped out of the car.

"Remember, we're all going to meet for dim sum at China Pearl on Sunday morning at ten o'clock. Please come if you can," Christie called after her.

Blair nodded, waved, and disappeared into the building. The car took off. As they turned the corner, Vicky looked back and saw Blair come out of the door she'd just entered, then run across the street. There was a small convenience store nearby. She must have forgotten to get something, Vicky thought. She was starting to wonder what it might have been when Teddy interrupted her musings. "Have you heard the latest MIT hack? You know they put a full-sized replica of one of the campus police cars on the dome awhile back?"

Christie laughed. "They're always doing stuff like that. The car looked totally real. They even had a dummy with a box of doughnuts in the front seat! What have the students done this time?"

"When I take you back to Cabot on Sunday, I'll show you. The dome looks like a giant beanie, complete with spinner on top. I have a lot of friends there, and yes, they are totally into their work, but they do have a sense of humor."

"Either that or go crazy," Maggie said, feeling very insightful. Maybe she could work this into a poem—humor to let off steam.

"I'm not your mother, but I think you're making a big mistake." Christie was trying hard not to lose her temper. It was the closest she had ever come to fighting with Maggie—or Vicky. The roommates had always been able to talk things out before too much steam built up. Not that they didn't get on one another's nerves occasionally, yet never anything major—until now.

"Exactly. You're *not* my mother, so quit acting like her. Amber only told me about the poetry reading this morning, and we left so fast, I didn't have a chance to ask Mrs. Babcox, and our housemother wasn't around."

Christie was sure Maggie hadn't looked too hard for either woman. Darn Amber St. James. She was doing some kind of body-snatching number on Maggie, and Christie was beginning to get seriously worried. She considered calling Vicky for help, only Maggie would just dig her heels in all the more. Christie herself would probably do the same in that situation; two against one was never a good idea. She took a deep breath.

"Look, Mags, what you decide is your business, but you know we're not allowed out on our own without an adult after dark on these weekends unless we get permission. My dad will be home from work soon and maybe we can all go together." Christie was pretty sure the last thing her father wanted to do at the end of the workweek was go to a poetry reading by undergraduates at a Harvard Square coffeehouse, yet he'd go, knowing how important it was to her.

"But the reading starts in an hour! Amber will be waiting. And she's going to introduce me to some of the poets!"

The aroma of strong coffee and incense filled the basement room. There wasn't an empty chair. All eyes were on the high stool under the spotlight at the front. Candles flickered on the small tables, casting curious shadows on the poster-covered walls.

"She's so young," someone whispered. "A remarkable talent," her companion said softly. "Reminiscent of Edna St. Vincent Millay. Even her name—Margaret St. Vincent Porter! A true 'Renascence!'"

The poet had slipped modestly into the room and was making her way toward the improvised stage, stopping now and then for a word with a friend or fan. A tall youth with tousled dark curls stood and handed her one perfect wine-colored rose. She held it to her nose and it seemed the whole room shared the strong scent, so obvious was her pleasure. She sat and began turning the pages of a large leather-bound notebook.

"I hope she reads 'Black Oak at Dawn.' It's my favorite," the woman who had spoken earlier said.

"Ssssh." The person at the next table was visibly annoyed. "You know she rarely does public readings. Tonight is my only chance!"

"My only chance!" Maggie said aloud, leaving her daydream behind. "Amber may never ask me again, especially if I don't go tonight. I really thought you'd understand." It was the old Maggie, her lower lip trembling.

And Christie did understand. She sighed. Oh Maggie, why are you so . . . so artistic! Christie said to herself. And what on earth am I going to do? The phone rang and her question was answered almost immediately.

"Sweetheart? I'll be tied up a little longer, sorry. Do you think you guys could order a pizza or something? I'll make it up to you tomorrow night. We'll take Maggie to Durgin Park or wherever you want."

"Don't worry. We're fine, and Durgin Park will be perfect. Maggie's seen the outside when we've been at the Faneuil Hall Marketplace, and we told her all about the huge portions and rude waitresses, except they're more funny than really rude." The last time

Christie had been there with her father, it had been after a diving meet, and she'd ordered the prime rib. When the waitress brought the huge piece of meat, she'd assumed it was for Cal Montgomery. When corrected, she said to Christie, "Whadda ya got under the table? Your Great Dane?"

"Okay, then, Durgin Park it will be. And I won't be late. Say 'hi' to Maggie. I'll see you both soon."

Christie hung up the phone and said, "My dad says hi and that he won't be home until later. We can order a pizza and go get some tapes. I'm in the mood for *Murder on the Orient Express* or maybe some of those old *Thin Man* movies." She was hoping desperately that Maggie would say yes. Little Bittern didn't have a Blockbuster Video, or anything remotely resembling one, Maggie had told them. The closest thing was a kind of lending library at the one and only market. She'd seen every James Bond movie ever made and *The Sound of Music* about thirty times. Ordinarily, a night of tapes would have had Maggie halfway out the door by now.

And Maggie did waver. The only pizza on Little Bittern was what her mom made, and it tended to be too good, not dripping with red sauce and loaded with pepperoni, but stuff like caramelized onions, prosciutto, and goat cheese. Pizza wasn't on the Cabot menu, either.

"Well . . ."

"After we get the tapes and food, we can get ready for bed and be like the girls in those books we used to read when we were younger who had pajama parties all the time. I've got some radical bloodred nail polish and we can do all our nails." Christie was running out of carrots to dangle in front of Maggie. She pitched her last one. "We can make s'mores."

Maggie shook her head slowly. "I'll be back before your dad gets home. I'm only going to stay a little while. The reading is early—it starts at six—because there's some kind of folk music stuff later. I'll be back before eight o'clock, I promise. But I can't miss this! How am I ever going to be a real writer if I don't hear what real writers have to say? It's a completely different experience hearing poetry read aloud than reading it." Maggie's voice had changed slightly at the end and Christie was pretty sure the business about hearing and reading poetry was a direct Amber quote.

"Do you know how to get there? And do you have the number here?"

Maggie looked peevish. "I'm not ten years old." Then she stopped and gave Christie a hug. "I'm sorry I sounded like a jerk. Yes and yes and I'll be safe and sound in your room before you know it." She was pulling on her jacket.

The door closed behind her. "If you're not, we could be in big trubs," Christie said to the thick oak panels.

But she wasn't back before Christie knew it. At seven, Christie had stationed herself at the bay window in the living room, which gave her a good view up and down Chestnut Street. It was too early to expect Maggie. The reading had been scheduled for six, but if

Maggie had had second thoughts about being there or—by some miracle—had become disenchanted with Amber, she could be walking up the street at any moment. The MBTA red line went directly from the Charles Street station, a short walk from the apartment, to Harvard Square. Trains ran frequently enough, so the trip could take as little as fifteen minutes, ten if you caught one immediately coming and going.

By eight o'clock, Christie was beginning to panic. Her father would certainly be home soon, and how was she going to explain where Maggie was? She didn't want to lie to her father, but she didn't want to get Maggie into trouble, either. For a moment, she was tempted to hop on the "T" herself and drag Maggie out of the reading, except she knew that that would only make things worse. Maybe the subway had broken down. This had been known to happen. Maybe at this very moment, Maggie was sitting in the dark somewhere underground between Harvard and Central squares. Christie didn't really believe this, though. The most likely scenario was Maggie sitting wide-eyed in adoration, totally oblivious of the time. Wake up, Mags. She wished she believed in telepathic communication. She sent the thought out a couple of times more just in case. Now she didn't dare leave the window. Every figure on the sidewalk made her heart race. If it was her father striding up the street, she'd have to do some quick thinking. If it was Maggie . . . well, she wasn't sure what she'd say first—"Glad you made it," or "Do you know how worried I've been! You could have called at least!" It sounded like something a parent would say. For a moment, she had to laugh. Then she stood close to the window again. Maggie! Where are you?

Maggie was becoming more and more uneasy. She had no idea what to do. The whole night wasn't turning out to be what she'd imagined at all.

First, the poets hadn't been exactly what she had expected. True, it was a reading and it was in a coffeehouse, but it turned out that it was a poetry-writing group, mainly Harvard undergraduates who met there to read and critique one another's work. Amber had introduced Maggie to everyone, then promptly ignored her, devoting her attentions to a guy with the same penchant for body piercing and black attire as Amber herself. His hair was shaved close to his scalp and his poetry was what one of the group admiringly referred to as "strong, earthy cries of rage." A young woman had read what Maggie thought were some moving, lyrical sonnets, but the group pronounced them "trite and imitative." Amber announced, "Too, too Edna St. Vincent Millay," and a few heads nodded. Then there was the coffee. Everyone was drinking endless caffe lattes, café mochas, cappuccinos, and espressos. Maggie didn't really like coffee, even the mocha, which had chocolate in it. Also, the prices were really high. Maggie was at Cabot on an alumnae scholarship, since her mother had gone there. The Porters had to watch every penny—watch most of them disappear into things like new plumbing for the inn—and Maggie didn't want to waste her money on something she didn't even want! She ordered a small cup and poured as much milk and sugar in as she could. She'd never been able to understand why something that smelled so good tasted so bad. She noticed that Amber had ordered a large latte, coffee with hot foamed milk, and was also dumping in sugar. Maybe she didn't like coffee, either. This observation made Maggie feel better. After all, here she was with people who were serious about their writing—and she was managing to drink coffee with them.

After the next person read, Maggie even offered a comment—a compliment on the use of alliteration. He smiled at her. "I like to make lists of words and phrases. I sing them out loud—mostly in the shower. 'On scrolls of silver snowy sentences,'" he recited dramatically. "That's from Hart Crane." Then everyone started giving examples and the group seemed more relaxed. Maggie was glowing, taking it all in. She looked across at Amber. She wasn't saying anything and she looked annoyed. No, Maggie corrected herself. It's just my imagination again. She's probably tired. Why would she be annoyed?

But after that brief moment, the group became intense again. Maggie looked at her watch. It was 7:45. She jumped up without hesitation.

She turned to Amber. "Sorry, I have to run. Thanks for telling me about it." A few heads nodded, and Maggie ran up the stairs out into the cold, dark night. She knew she hadn't wanted to stay any longer, but what she hadn't figured out was why not.

She dashed to the station and bounded onto the train as the doors were closing. Mr. Montgomery would certainly not be home this early, and if he was . . . well, she'd say . . . what *would* she say?

She'd been so intent on going to Harvard Square for the reading that she hadn't really thought about the consequences.

Screech! The train slammed to a halt after entering the tunnel. A man's briefcase went sliding down the car, slamming up against the door to the next one. Then the lights went out.

"And Dad's bound to be back any minute. What am I going to tell him?"

At 8:15, Christie had called Vicky, leaving her post only for an instant to get the phone. Talking, she was still scanning the sidewalks, as she'd been doing for over an hour.

Vicky sighed. This was so unlike Maggie. And so unfair. Christie could get in a lot of trouble, too. But now to avoid it . . .

"Is there any way you could kind of let him think Maggie was upstairs without coming out and saying so?"

"Well," Christie said slowly, "he'll assume she's with me in my room watching a video or something. Maybe I won't have to say anything. If I see him coming, I could just run upstairs and call down to him. 'Be there in a minute,' except I haven't seen him in a couple of weeks and—"

"No," Vicky said, cutting her off. Christie and her

dad were still working through a lot of things. Cal Montgomery had always been at the office late, traveling frequently. Christie's mother had been the parent at home, at Christie's meets, and on vacations. The last thing father and daughter needed now was for father not to be greeted warmly and immediately by daughter, who sincerely wanted to. Vicky was really getting mad at Maggie. What could the girl have been thinking of!

"Look, keep talking to me. Maybe we'll get lucky. Maybe Mags will turn the corner any second."

"And maybe I'll be pulling Santa's sleigh next year," Christie said glumly.

"So I asked my mother what had happened to Grandmother—you noticed, didn't you? The woman looks like the 'after' picture in one of those megavitamin ads. Anyway, from the way Mom snapped at me, it was like I had asked some terribly offensive question. She should have just said it was none of my business, but instead, she said my grandmother looked exactly the same as always and that, as usual, I was too concerned with appearances. 'Better to concentrate on things that matter.'" Vicky and Christie were still talking, and to distract her friend while she was waiting, Vicky had mentioned the conversation with her mother. One of their typical nonconversations was how Vicky thought of it.

"But there's nothing wrong with your grandmother. Just the opposite. I haven't seen her many times, but I *did* think she looked very healthy and . . . well, rosy. So you mother can't be worried about her. It must be something else that happened to come out when you were talking about this."

"It's always something else, or rather something. Any excuse to bite my head off," Vicky said bitterly.

"Why don't you talk to Teddy?"

"Now, that's sensible advice," Vicky said, and resolved to call her cousin in the morning. "Okay, we've solved one thing. Now where the heck is Maggie!"

Maggie's first impulse was to scream, and someone did let out a startled cry. Then the lights flickered and went back on. Everyone looked slightly abashed to be in the light again. Maggie relaxed, waiting for the drone of the engine. But it didn't come. "Second time this week," a man across the aisle said. The minutes ticked by. Maggie knew what people with claustrophobia must feel like. She felt trapped, buried alive, no way to get out. She forced herself to stay focused. This was no time for one of her daydreams. Nightmare. It's a nightmare, she kept saying to herself. Mr. Montgomery will have to tell Mrs. Babcox and she'll tell my parents and I'll be grounded for the rest of my life, or maybe asked to leave Cabot, or . . . Her eyes were filling up with tears. Stupid! she yelled at herself. She knew what she was doing was wrong, but she hadn't listened. It was as if there were two Maggies all of a sudden and the one who wanted to go to Harvard Square had drowned out the other one.

The train started with what was, to Maggie, a deafening roar, then lurched down the tracks. First Central Square, next Kendall, and finally the train was above ground and crossing the Charles River, lying dark and murky below the bridge. She flew out the doors as soon as they opened and raced down the platform to the stairs that led to Charles Street. It was 8:35.

Never had the street seemed so long and so crowded. The lights were against her at every crosswalk. Finally, Chestnut was directly ahead of her.

And so was Mr. Montgomery.

🐉 Chapter Four

Maggie froze. There was no way she could get past Christie's father and into the house. But there was a rear entrance. . . .He'd go in the front door and she could go through the back, only it was sure to be locked. And how could she let Christie know she was there? Even if there was a bell, she couldn't ring it!

There weren't very many people on the sidewalk at this end of Charles Street. Mr. Montgomery had stopped to let a car go by before crossing. What if he looked over his shoulder or decided to turn back for a newspaper or something? She had to get out of here—and fast. She darted into a doorway, watched him turn the corner toward his house, then sped to a 7-Eleven she'd passed. It had a phone. Quickly, she dialed Christie's number. She let it ring, heard the answering machine, hung up, and dialed again. The same thing happened. It was no use. No one was home.

Where was Christie!

When Christie saw her father walking up the steep sidewalk, all her indecision had vanished. She had slammed the phone down on a bewildered Vicky, then grabbed her parka and hastily scribbled a note, putting it on the floor in front of the door, where he wouldn't miss it.

Dad—

Went for ice cream. Be back soon.

Love you,
Christie

Strictly speaking, they shouldn't even be going such a short distance at this hour, but she couldn't think of any other way out of this mess.

Then she went down the back stairs into their tiny garden and through the door in the brick wall that led to the side street, Spruce Street. Beacon Hill looked especially beautiful. The old brick town houses stood silently in the gentle glow from the gas streetlights. Many of them still had the original early-nineteenth century wavy glass windowpanes that decades of sunlight had turned purple. A lamp shining through one sent amethyst streaks into the night. Doorways, roofs, and the high walls that kept prying eyes from yards were topped with snow—thin lines of icing, partly melted from the warmth of the day.

Looking about her at the familiar surroundings, she took a deep breath. Now all she had to do was find Maggie—and get some ice cream.

She took Spruce to Beacon and walked down toward

the Public Garden, which was across the street from the Boston Common. The swan boats were in storage for the winter, but the bronze statues of Quack and the other ducklings from Robert McCloskey's book braved the elements. At the intersection, she turned right on Charles. It was unlikely her father would be looking out the window down Chestnut Street, the way he'd come, but better not to take the chance. She was feeling angry again—angry at Amber, with her pretentious, phony ways, and angry at Maggie for getting so caught up in them. She and Vicky had to do something, but what? They all had other friends. She'd made some through diving; some were from her old school. Vicky hung out with the Drama Club crowd. Yet there had never been any conflict. She shivered. She'd come to depend on being the threesome they were, Christie & Company. What if it got destroyed forever?

At her wit's end, Maggie had decided the only thing to do was to go to Christie's house, ring the bell, and hope she answered. Maybe Christie had been in the shower, or maybe the TV kept her from hearing the phone. Maybe . . . At this point, she didn't care. She couldn't stay out on the street all night. She couldn't go back to school or to Vicky's. How could she explain to Mr. and Mrs. Lee why she wasn't at the Montgomerys'? There was no other choice. Stupid, stupid, stupid! She walked slowly down Charles Street. She knew she was about to cry, so she kept her eyes focused on the slushy sidewalk beneath her. Suddenly, someone grabbed her. Her head jerked up.

"Christie!"

"Oh Maggie, I've been so worried about you!"

The two girls hugged each other hard.

"My father was almost home. I've been watching out the window. . . ."

"I know! He was right in front of me. If that stupid train hadn't broken down, I would have made it!" Maggie was indignant. Christie didn't say anything, but the feeling in her stomach that had started to go away came back.

"Well," she said reluctantly, "I left him a note saying that we went out for ice cream, so we'd better hurry and get some."

"That was brilliant," Maggie said, enormously relieved. "Hercule Poirot couldn't have done any better."

Oh yes he could, Christie said to herself bitterly as they walked across the street to get cones at Rebecca's Bakery in a corner of the old Charles Street Meeting House. She couldn't believe Maggie was smiling as if nothing had happened. Everything had turned out all right. Thank goodness for Christie! her expression read.

The din surrounding them made conversation difficult. Maggie, Christie, and Vicky were sitting at a large round table on the main floor of the China Pearl restaurant in Chinatown. It was pleasantly warm, partly from all the people consuming the steaming food, and partly from the feeling the bright red-and-gold decor gave the diners. Across from them were a young couple, an older couple, and an infant in a stroller, sound asleep. The girls had saved a place for Blair and had taken seats facing the top of the stairs that led to the restaurant, so they would have no trouble spotting her among the people who stood holding their numbered tickets, patiently waiting. Vicky had told them to get there early, but they had still had to wait and watch all sorts of delicious-looking things stacked on carts roll past. The cries of the women pushing the carts punctuated the steady, happy drone of those eating.

"What are they saying?" Maggie asked, raising her own voice to be heard.

"What they have on the cart—*char siu bau*—she's got steamed pork buns," Vicky answered, pointing toward a woman making her way slowly past the tables.

"What is this? It's delicious," Christie said into Vicky's ear.

"*Har gau*—steamed shrimp dumplings," Vicky told her. "I'm waiting for the braised chicken feet."

Christie made a face. "Real feet!"

Vicky nodded. "They're wonderful. At least try one if I can get us a dish. You eat wings, don't you?" Privately, she thought that American cooking wasted the best part of most animals. She wouldn't push another of her favorites—a tripe dish—on her friends, at least not today. She'd feel she'd accomplished something if they would each take a taste of the chicken feet, crunchy and covered with a spicy sauce.

"I'm afraid Blair isn't coming," Christie said, spearing a pork dumpling that looked like a tiny fluffy white pillow with her chopstick.

Vicky turned the lid of their teapot upside down to indicate that they needed more tea, then scanned the carts with a practiced eye. No chicken feet yet, but one was approaching with turnip cakes—the vegetable ground fine, shaped into a rectangle, and then quickly fried right at the table on a grill built into the cart.

The words *Dim sum* mean "touch the heart," a shortened version of the original Chinese phrase meaning "ordering the dish following your heart or inclination." This was the part Vicky loved. You never knew what a cart might hold, and you merely pointed to a dish that attracted you at the moment and it was yours. The waiter then stamped a card on the table. Vicky had planned the meal carefully for her friends, starting with sweet sticky rice that had been wrapped in a lotus leaf and steamed. Buried in the rice when you opened the bundle were tiny pieces of chicken, Chinese sausage, and maybe a quail egg. It symbolized the whole dim sum experience—tasty little treasures.

She looked across the table at the family enjoying its time together. As was customary, the younger people were offering the dishes first to the older couple— his parents, her parents? The baby slept on, oblivious of the noise and motion. Dim sum is not really a meal you can eat alone, Vicky thought. Even if she wanted the food, it would never occur to her to come by herself. You came with friends. The men and women at the next table were discussing business—more pleasant this way than around a conference table in an office. The Ginger Jar offered dim sum on Sundays, but it catered to Western tastes—plenty of buns, pot stickers, scallion pancakes, things like that. The Sunday chef, who only did dim sum, could make anything, but the Lees had discovered what their clientele liked, and they stuck with it.

"There she is!" Maggie called, and rushed over to Blair, who was standing near the cash register, an anxious look on her face. She was carrying two enormous bundles wrapped in brown paper and tied with string.

Christie watched Maggie go. It hadn't been the best weekend. Appearing with their ice cream Friday night, they had been warmly greeted by Mr. Montgomery. Maggie went upstairs to Christie's room to watch TV and Christie sat up talking with her dad, feeling guilty even though she really hadn't done anything. By the time she got to her room, Maggie was asleep in the other bed—or pretending to be. Christie assumed she was embarrassed and upset about the whole night. She figured Maggie would tell her all about it in the morning, and then this feeling that Maggie was drifting away from her would be exposed for the nonsense it was. But Maggie slept late and adroitly avoided any heart-to-heart talks. Instead, she insisted on walking all over "the Hill," even going back inside the gold-domed State House at the pinnacle, although they'd done it last fall. They'd ended up at Vicky's favorite haunt—Filene's Basement. Maggie wore her purchase to dinner at Durgin Park that night—a pair of jet black jeans. They were a bargain, but Maggie had used her whole month's spending money. Christie had kept her mouth shut—something that was getting to be a habit around Maggie. She didn't want to sound like Maggie's mother again, but what if Maggie needed money for something? Well, at least she'd get a lot of wear out of the pants. She was wearing them again today. Christie sighed.

Vicky picked up on her friend's mood immediately. She swallowed a mouthful of the chicken feet. After one polite taste, her friends had left the dish to her. "They really do look like a chicken's foot!" Maggie had exclaimed. "Talons and all!" Vicky was pretty sure she knew what was bothering Christie. It was bothering her, too. With Maggie off telling Blair where they were sitting, Vicky grabbed the chance to talk. Christie had made a quick call Friday night to say Maggie had returned, but they hadn't discussed what had happened.

"What's up? You haven't been yourself all morning. Is it Maggie?"

Christie nodded. "It's stupid, and I should just come right out and tell her what's on my mind. I guess I'm still mad about Friday night, or mad that she doesn't seem to realize the position she put me in—or herself. I mean, it's not like I'm some Miss Perfect, only Maggie could have gotten suspended!"

"I know. But I don't think she's ready to hear anything from us. Amber has caught her in her web and Maggie's the perfect fly. It won't last. She's still our

Maggie, and after awhile, she'll see Amber for what she is. Or Amber will get bored with Maggie. Either way, we're here to catch her."

"You're right, but it's a pain in the neck mean-while." Christie frowned.

Maggie and Blair had managed to stow the parcels on the coatrack, and now they sat down.

"I didn't think I would make it!"

"You didn't get lost, did you?" Vicky teased.

Blair smiled good-naturedly. "Not here. No, I had to wait for my mother to finish, and I can't stay long. I must take these to her boss."

"On a Sunday!" Maggie exclaimed.

"My mother works every day," Blair said, and Maggie flushed. It was obvious that with Mr. Chan gone, Mrs. Chan must be under a lot of pressure to support her family. It reminded Maggie of something, and the question came popping out.

"You never told us how you ended up at Cabot."

Vicky was pouring tea in Blair's cup and offering her some of the chicken feet. "More things will be coming around soon. I want some dessert."

"No thank you. Just some tea. I have eaten already," Blair said, declining politely. Vicky pointed to a dish with three egg-custard tarts and the three girls, between bites, looked expectantly at their new friend.

"It was Mrs. Blair Samuels," Blair said. "All the time she was teaching me English, she kept telling me about Cabot. I felt as if I were there sometimes. It was so real to me. Cabot was her old school—she was a student with Mrs. Babcox—and Mrs. Samuels is on the Cabot board of trustees. We both had dreams that I would go there. Except when I got here, my father was sick and my mother needed me. Until now, she could not spare me."

"But you went to school, didn't you?" Christie asked.

"Yes, of course. We arrived in November. It was very cold. My school was not far from the apartment, only it seemed a long way."

Blair didn't want to talk about the old school. It was large, overcrowded, and she had felt depressed about being there. She longed to stay home and help take care of her father, studying the books on her own. Most of what she had been doing in her classes, she already knew. It was hard to make friends. Everybody seemed to be in cliques based on where you lived and who you were. There was no place for her, even among the new arrivals from Asia, because her English was so good. She didn't need classes in English as a second language, and the ESL kids, as they were known, mistakenly thought her a snob because of her abilities. She made one or two friends, outsiders like herself, worked to make good grades, and waited to go to Cabot.

"I had hoped to come last fall, but my father died in August, just after Mason was born. I couldn't start until now, and it has definitely been worth the wait. I love being at Cabot!"

Maggie was acting like her old self, her insatiable curiosity prompting her to ask questions. "Mason?

That's an unusual name. Why did your parents choose it?"

Vicky smiled. She knew the answer, but she let Blair reply. "His Chinese name is Meǐ Shēng. Meǐ is the name for America and *sen* means 'born'; it sounds like the name, Shēng. All Chinese names have meanings, especially for good luck. My brother had the good luck to be born here. He is a citizen, and Mason is the closest English name we could find. I took the book of baby names out of the library. It said Mason means 'stoneworker,' and my mother's grandfather did that, so we knew it was the right name for lots of reasons."

Maggie wished she had a more interesting name than Margaret. Christie had a name with a history, and so did Vicky. Her real name was Victoria, and it represented her parents' "victory" at having a child and leaving Hong Kong to start a new life with her. Margaret was just something her parents thought sounded good with Porter. She'd change it when she was older, maybe something like Deidre, or Calliope, the ancient Greek Muse of epic poetry. "Cali" for short—or "Cal," not "Cal," Calvin Montgomery! She didn't want to think about that episode now.

Blair was still talking about her little brother. "He was born in August, just when the first moon cakes went on sale. The Moon Festival in the middle of August is a very important holiday for us."

Vicky nodded. "It's a little bit like Thanksgiving. Your whole family comes to one house, only instead of turkey, you eat moon cakes."

"Moon cakes?" Christie was picturing something made of green cheese, and she almost laughed.

"They're delicious," Vicky said. "My parents order individual ones from a place in San Francisco, because they say they're the closest to the ones they remember from their own childhoods, and I'm not complaining. The cakes are like pastries, very flaky and round like the moon. Inside, they're filled with all sorts of yummy things: sweet pastes of lotus seeds, pineapples, dates, or red beans. And they're so pretty; the dough turns gold after it's baked and the mold the cake is baked in leaves a character on the cake that tells you what's inside or symbolizes Chang E, the Moon Lady."

"Pineapple is my favorite," Blair said. "We had a large one that everyone shared. Father was still alive, and we watched the August moon together and made our wishes. It was my only time to watch the moon with him. Each year in Taiwan, we put out his chopsticks, and we will again next August."

"You set a place for anyone who can't come or who has died," Vicky explained.

Christie liked the idea. "Like toasting absent friends at New Year's."

"Exactly—and, speaking of which, don't forget next Sunday you're all invited to the banquet at the restaurant after we watch the Lion Dances here. My parents would like you, your mother, and brother to join us, too, Blair. We have it on Sunday instead of New Year's Eve, because of the restaurant. We'll be too busy Saturday night doing Chinese New Year banquets for other families."

Blair looked perturbed. "I will ask. . . ." She didn't make any promises. Maggie began to wonder why Blair seemed so worried today. It was a big change from the confused but happy student she'd been all week.

"Mags, come back to us. Blair has to go, and we thought we'd help her take the stuff to the warehouse." Christie's voice sliced into Maggie's reverie.

A waiter came and counted up the empty dishes on the table and the stamps on the card he'd given them when they sat down. The people on the other side were still eating—clams in a fragrant black bean sauce now. The baby was awake and smiling happily, waving one tiny fist around.

"I can't wait to see Mason," Maggie said. "Do you think we could?"

Blair looked a little worried. It was how she had looked when Maggie first spotted her. "Of course," she said, "but today is not a good time. He's . . . he's a little fussy today, maybe getting teeth."

"Oh, I didn't mean today," Maggie reassured her.

Out on the sidewalk, Blair was adamant about taking the bundles alone, and after a moment or two of her insisting, Vicky said, "If you're sure, we'll start back. See you at school tomorrow." They waved goodbye. Impulsively, Blair called after the girls. "Thank you! For all your help at school, for . . ." The three waved again and Christie called, "That's what friends are for!"

"Let's take some pastries back for Aisha and Imani. They love Chinese food," Christie suggested as they walked past a bakery with a tempting array in the window.

"Great idea," Maggie agreed. "But why did you let Blair leave, Vicky? That stuff is incredibly heavy. It was hard to get it up on the rack in the restaurant."

"I know, except she really didn't want us to go with her. You only know this part of Chinatown—and the places all three of us go in Boston are pretty limited. The warehouse and the workers there are parts of Blair's life she wants to keep separate. Chinese people are very big on saving face, and I was picking up on that loud and clear."

"Saving face"—it reminded Christie of this whole thing with Maggie. Maybe Maggie really *did* feel bad but couldn't talk about it. The thought made her feel better.

The bundles filled with the completed piecework her mother had worked on in their tiny apartment *were* heavy. By the time Blair got to her destination, her shoulders were aching. She and her mother had looped the string so she could carry them on her back. Now the string was cutting cruelly into her hands, right through her thin woolen gloves. It would have been easier to hang the packages from a pole across her shoulders, but she hadn't seen anyone carrying things like that in this country, and Blair did not want to stand out. She pushed a buzzer by the loading dock. After a long wait, a man came and took the work, speaking to her roughly in Chinese. She told him how many shirts were in each and he disappeared, returning with a slip of paper and the total amount of money Mrs. Chan was owed.

"But this is not right!" Blair protested. "Please count them."

"I did count them," he replied, and walked down the concrete stairs to where she was standing. Blair felt afraid, yet she did not run.

"Then please, could you count them again?" she said, trying to keep her voice from shaking. The man was standing very close to her. He smelled of cigarettes and something else, a sour smell.

"I said I counted them." He raised his hand.

This time, she ran.

Rounding the corner, she stopped short. Vicky, Christie, and Maggie were right in front of her, carrying two white cartons.

"Hi, Blair!" Maggie called out, apparently oblivious to the fear and hesitation on the girl's face. But Vicky noticed, and so did Christie. They hastened forward.

"Are you okay?" Christie asked. She recalled what Vicky had just said about respecting Blair's privacy, but the girl looked as if she'd seen a ghost or something.

"I was running," Blair stammered. "I got—how do you say it? A pain here, in the side."

"A stitch in your side," Maggie answered. "A pretty graphic image!"

Blair forced a smile. "It must have been a large needle, but I am fine now. Sorry I can't stay to talk, but my mother is waiting." She waved and was off again, walking rapidly.

Christie looked after her. She knew what a stitch in your side felt like, and maybe Blair had had one, but something else was going on. She could tell from looking at Vicky that she was thinking the same thing. Their new friend might feel thrilled to be at Cabot, presenting her cheerful, self-confident self to that world, but in this one, there was another Blair. And Christie intended to find out who that girl was and what was scaring her to death.

🐉 Chapter Five

The two and a half days off campus had not provided Christie & Company with the relaxed break it had apparently given other Cabot students. Aisha and Imani Brooks, fellow Widow residents, were bubbling over with all the fun they'd had at home over the weekend. Marine Collonges, Christie's Cabot Guide, was with them. She spent so much time studying that it was unusual for her to take a break, and they'd all been happy that she'd come up to the third floor.

Imani was devouring a pork bun, "Girl," she said to Vicky, "you look like you've got the weight of the world pressing down on you, instead of a few days out of here. What's going on?"

It was hard to answer. On the one hand, the visit home had been great, if slightly bewildering. She had not been able to get her grandmother to tell her why she looked so much better. Vicky had asked in any number of ways: "Are you taking a new medicine, Grandmother? Have you discovered the magic fountain of youth, Grandmother?" Her grandmother had laughed at them all and denied any difference in her appearance. Not daring to raise the subject again with her mother, Vicky had approached her father. Surely he would have noticed the change in his own mother's appearance! But Mr. Lee merely said, "Oh, yes, grandmother looks fine. She always looks fine." Vicky hadn't seen her cousin Teddy after Friday night. Mr. Lee had driven them back to Cabot, because Teddy had to study for an exam. But she was more resolved than ever to ask Teddy what he thought. She was sure he'd have noticed the change. Old Mrs. Lee even seemed to move more easily. Yet her grandmother's good health was not something to worry about. Could the old lady have a boyfriend? A new lease on life!

No, it was not her grandmother's mysterious bright complexion that worried her, but the same old problem that confronted Vicky whenever she was with her mother. Even after the unpleasant exchange about old Mrs. Lee, Vicky had hoped she and her mother would be able to spend some time together, and she'd kept all Saturday clear. In the morning, she had suggested they do something, just the two of them. There was an exhibit of Chinese ceramics at the Museum of Fine Arts, and Mrs. Lee was very knowledgeable on the subject. But when Vicky brought it up, her mother had said she was too busy to go. So Vicky stayed and helped at the restaurant, conscious of what a slow day it was until late in the afternoon. They could have gone. He mother had obviously not wanted to go with her.

"It's my mother again," she told Imani. "She never talks to me. She . . . well, it's complicated."

"I wish our mother was a little more like that," Aisha complained. "It's like our lives are hers forever. She wants details, details, details, and forget about doing any serious partying. The only way we're going to get to go anywhere until we're thirty is if she or my father goes with us!"

"But you have fun with her," Maggie pointed out. "You're always talking about going to her openings and about all the people who come round your house." The Brooks family lived in Boston's South End, and Mrs. Brooks worked organizing exhibitions of African-American art. Mr. Brooks was an architect.

"She *is* a fun lady," Aisha admitted, "but she's still a mother and, by definition, a nuisance." As she said it, she was aware of Christie nibbling a dumpling, comfortably curled up on the couch next to her. Losing your mother—or father—Aisha hoped it would never happen to them.

A girl appeared at the door. "You have a phone call, Maggie."

Maggie flew out of the room. Every once in awhile, her parents called on Sunday nights with news of Little Bittern. Cabot had been the right choice, but Maggie still longed to hear the cry of gulls when she woke up in the morning. The tidy campus with its acres of trees made her feel landlocked.

She was back soon.

"Guess what!" Her face was radiant. "That was Amber, and she asked me if I'd go over some of the things she's working on for class! Kind of a peer review."

Christie didn't want to pop Maggie's bubble, yet she couldn't help saying, "I thought the class as a group went over things."

"They do, but she wants to get a head start. I can hardly wait. We're meeting at her dorm tomorrow afternoon." She twirled around, ending up at the window.

The other girls looked at one another. Aisha said softly, "Peer review, my sweet aunt, as Dad says. Miss Amber wants to pick Maggie's brains, and afterward Maggie will be lucky to have any of her own ideas left!"

"And I thought she was mad at me on Friday night," Maggie said, rejoining the group. "It just goes to show how wrong you can be."

"Yes indeed," Vicky said emphatically.

The weather all week was unseasonably warm. Maggie was working on a poem in the small study room on Widow's first floor, just off the common room, which had been the dining room when each house had its own. Maggie imagined that this little cozy room with only one small window had probably been some kind of a butler's pantry. Outside, the sun was melting the snow from the roof and a steady *drip, drip, drip* punctuated Maggie's thoughts.

"Oh, Mr. Hudson, whatever do you think they will do about Lady Margaret! She's gone and done it this time, that girl!"

"Now, Mrs. Bridges, it's not our place to pass judgment on things that go on upstairs. You'd do better to concentrate on his Lordship's dinner. Still, I do admit it will take some time for life here to settle back to normal after this poetry book the young mistress has published. I had to chase another of those newspaper reporters away from the door this morning!"

"I can't even understand half of what the words mean!"

"And better you shouldn't, my dear, better you shouldn't." Hudson flushed at the memory of certain lines. Descriptions of her Ladyship's feelings for nature that sounded . . . well, a wee bit earthy.

Drip, drip, drip.

It wasn't a leaky faucet in the scullery, but the melting snow hitting the windowsill. Maggie reluctantly left her *Masterpiece Theatre* daydream and returned to her poem. She'd been spending so much time helping Amber with *her* writing that when Maggie grabbed a minute for her own, all her thoughts seemed to disappear. Plus, she was getting confused about which were her ideas and which were Amber's. She wondered if Elizabeth Barrett Browning, another of her favorites, had ever had this problem. After all, her husband, Robert, had been a poet, too, and they must have read each other's work, made suggestions. Still, it wasn't working for her—this collaboration, or whatever it was. She wished Amber had never asked her. There, the thought was out. But how could she tell her new friend she didn't want to help her anymore? She also wished she could ask Vicky and Christie for advice, yet whenever she mentioned Amber or the writing class, they changed the subject. Maggie felt stubborn suddenly. The two Maggies of last Friday night were back. Her friends were probably a little jealous of Amber, who was definitely cool. And if she needed some feedback on her work, then Maggie should feel honored that Amber St. James had picked her.

"Did you see Blair today?" Vicky asked her roommates. It was Wednesday night and she was coming back from the library. "She wasn't in English or social studies."

Christie shook her head. "Maggie and I looked for her at lunch. We knew you were going to be late. She didn't eat with you?"

Since arriving at Cabot, Blair had eaten with at least one of the girls every day. Her comments on the strictly Western fare served up by the Cabot cafeteria had broken them up more than once. "Why do they call this 'American chop suey'? It has macaroni in it. And chop suey is American anyway. It was invented here. And what are these?" She had been pointing to a bowl of croutons for their salads. "Little squares of old bread? A snack? Like popcorn?"

Now Vicky answered Christie's question. "No, but she was here yesterday. I hope she's not sick."

"That would be a shame—to miss school when she's just started. She'd hate to get behind. Why don't we ask the housemother? If Blair's sick, she'll know.

There would have been a call." Day students had lockers at Widow and were responsible to the housemother, just as the boarders were.

"I'll go," Maggie volunteered. She felt better than she had all week. The battle of the two Maggies was over, at least for the present. Shortly before dinner, Amber had asked her to come over to her dorm for some last-minute editing and Maggie number one, as Maggie was beginning to think of her, had politely but firmly declined, explaining that she had to study for a math test. Amber had simply said, "Whatever," so everything was fine. This was how Amber always talked.

Maggie was back soon. "No call. We probably just missed her at lunch, although, come to think of it, she wasn't in science. Where was she during all those classes? The infirmary?"

"Have you noticed that she didn't seem as excited to be here as she was last week?" Christie asked. "Maybe she was coming down with something, or maybe it's something else, something about the place that's bothering her."

"I have noticed," Vicky said, "and I've really been a rotten guide, but it's hard to know when to intrude. Blair and I really do come from a very different culture than the one you guys do. We're not 'let it all hang out' people."

Vicky always thought of herself as Chinese-American, with the emphasis on *American*. She was an infant when she left Hong Kong, so this was the only country she knew, despite close ties to the Chinese community and the fact that her family *was* a traditional one, especially in Vicky's eyes. Yet, since meeting Blair, the Chinese part was getting a whole lot more attention. Part of it was Mrs. Lee's obvious approval of Blair. But Vicky also found herself thinking with pride of their customs, like the Autumn Moon Festival in August and the upcoming New Year. Still, she knew that her American roots were healthy ones and wished she could convince her mother that expressing your opinion, even dressing in your own way, wasn't disrespectful. Maybe there were two Vickys. She found the idea confusing. If she acted and dressed more like Blair, would her mother talk to her?

"I don't think the cultures are all that different," Christie pointed out. "My background is pretty much solid WASP, you know, white Anglo-Saxon Protestant, and expressing feelings is simply not done, don't you know." She said the last in an affected voice, pushing the tip of her nose up. The girls laughed. Christie added, "It was really hard when Mom first got sick, because no one would talk about it. My grandparents still have a hard time, and I know how upset they are. Mom always said she married Dad to get some new Irish blood into the family. Not wanting to pry into Blair's life may have something to do with the traditions of your culture, but I think the kind of friend you want to be is your own choice—no matter where your great-great-grandparents came from!"

"Another job for Christie and Company," said Maggie, who had been intently absorbing Christie's words. Her own family, with the exception of Maggie, she liked to think, never kept things in, even if you wanted them to. Maybe that wasn't quite the burden she'd thought it was—although her mom's reputation for being the eagle eye of every neighborhood they'd lived in had been a tough one for her daughter.

"Tomorrow we check all her classes." Maggie got out her notebook. "We know her schedule, and if she isn't here, we track her down. She must have a phone."

"The problem will be getting the number. There are bound to be a million Chans in the Boston phone book, and we don't know what her father's name was. Why didn't I ask her for her number? I haven't been thinking!" Vicky wailed.

"I'm sure she'll be here tomorrow," Christie said, "and we can all have a big laugh about this."

They went to bed, but it was a long time before all the girls were asleep. Vicky heard both her roommates tossing and turning before she was slowly pulled into unconsciousness herself. Her last image was of Blair's frightened face when they'd run into her after she had delivered her mother's work.

Bì Yún "Blair" Chan wasn't at Cabot on Thursday, either. The girls met at lunch. Aisha and Imani Brooks joined them.

"We're kind of concerned, because Blair hasn't been in school yesterday or today," Christie explained. "And the housemother said she hadn't gotten word that she was sick. We checked the infirmary and they didn't know anything, either."

"Why don't you ask Mrs. Babcox?" Aisha suggested.

"I'm going to try to see her after my last class," Vicky said. "I'm sure she'll know, and if she doesn't, she should!"

"Now calm down, and let's get serious," Imani said. "What are we wearing for the dance tomorrow night? It's supposed to be casual, a pizza party, but I don't want to be the only one in jeans and a sweatshirt."

Maggie had forgotten all about the dance with Mansfield Hill Academy, although earlier in the week, they had teased Christie about Scott Franklin, an eighth grader who was on Mansfield's diving team. He was just a friend, Christie insisted, but she did own up to liking his phone calls, and they always sat together on the bus when the schools were attending the same meets. Scott felt the same way about diving that she did. It was when she was happiest, and all the training, the hard work, was part of it. Her roommates frequently talked about their future plans. Maggie's were literary, of course. Vicky was interested in a career in science—environmental chemistry. They were already focused. Entering the water without making a splash after flying through the air with a feeling of freedom she never experienced on solid ground was all she wanted to focus on now. Christie didn't want to think about the future yet—or the past.

"I'm wearing my new black jeans," Maggie said.

"Just don't be getting holes pierced all over your

body, Mags. Your ears are enough," Imani, Maggie's Cabot Guide, advised. "I have a friend who did her nose and then got a cold and—" The girls shrieked and threatened to throw Jell-O cubes at her.

"Don't get carried away is all," Imani finished when they'd stopped laughing.

Maggie hadn't been laughing quite as hard as the rest, and now she said, "I have no intention of wearing a ring in my nose." Her tone sounded a bit testy.

Christie and Vicky looked at each other over Maggie's head as their roommate bent over her tray to eat the last of her lunch. But she didn't say she wouldn't have anything else done, they telegraphed to each other.

"Are you and Mark "the Babe" Reese still an item?" Aisha asked Vicky. Mark Reese was a tenth grader at Mansfield and had been cast with Vicky in the Drama Club's production of Arthur Miller's *The Crucible* last fall.

"Well, I do know he's planning to go on Friday, but I'm not sure *item* is the right word. Anyway, I'm wearing jeans and probably the red velvet jacket I got in that rummage sale we went to—you know, at the First Parish Church on the green in busy downtown Aleford."

Sleepy Aleford, which did not even have a Gap store or a CVS, was not Vicky's idea of a place to live. Okay for school, but she planned to be out of here forever come graduation. Maggie, on the other hand, loved to wander in Aleford's conservation land and thought Main Street was perfect.

The girls hurried away, and as the afternoon shadows lengthened, Vicky found her thoughts turning with increasing frequency to Blair. There was only one phone, except for the housemother's, at Widow and Vicky knew Blair had the numbers of both. She had fulfilled at least some of her Guide duties. Why hadn't Blair called? She must know they would worry.

This time, Vicky knew why she was going to the headmistress's office, and she told the secretary she'd like to see Mrs. Babcox.

"Oh, I'm sorry, you just missed her, and she won't be back until tomorrow night—in time for the dance. Is it something I can help you with?"

Vicky hesitated. She had really wanted to talk to the headmistress herself, since Mrs. Babcox knew all about Blair and the connection to Mrs. Samuels, her old schoolmate. She hesitated. "Well, I haven't seen my friend Blair, Blair Chan, the new eighth grader, and I wondered if she was sick or something."

The secretary, Mrs. Watson, was a large, cheerful woman with a slightly booming voice, "There *is* a nasty flu around, but your friend doesn't have it or we would have been notified. The housemothers send a list of absences to the infirmary and we get a copy. I remember Blair very well, of course. She's probably holed up in the library, trying to keep her head above water. It can't be easy for her, coming here in the middle of the year." She shuffled some papers on her desk, and Vicky realized the woman must have work to do herself. She thanked her and left. Maybe Blair had panicked about the academic load and was cutting classes to study in the library, or some other place on campus. They all had their favorites for crunch times, when things in their own room were distracting. She felt better. And Mrs. Babcox would be back tomorrow night. If Blair was still missing, Vicky would corner the headmistress at the dance. An image of do-si-doing with the ramrod-straight gray-haired administrator flashed into Vicky's mind. She was getting to be as bad a daydreamer as Maggie.

Maggie. At first, the following day, Christie and Vicky could not even say their friend's name out loud. Then they found their voices and screamed in unison, "Maggie! What happened!"

Maggie was crying so hard, she couldn't answer. She looked at her friend's faces and buried her face in her pillow. They rushed over to her.

"Come on, tell us what happened!" Vicky insisted, patting Maggie's back.

Maggie lifted her puffy, tear-streaked face.

"Amber gave me a haircut," she managed to whisper before the sobs started again.

Chapter Six

"**W**hat do you mean, Amber cut your hair!" Vicky was furious. It was more like Amber had taken a lawn mower or a chain saw to Maggie's beautiful shoulder-length reddish brown curls. Now the hair was an uneven chin length on one side and earlobe length on the other. Bangs snaked crookedly across Maggie's brow. And the back! Maggie's thick wavy locks had fought whatever blunt instrument Ms. St. James had used, and there was a series of odd tufts reaching to the top of Maggie's T-shirt.

"I can't leave this room for months!" Maggie cried.

Vicky was inclined to agree with her. She instinctively patted her own long, gleaming hair. But, of course, Maggie couldn't entomb herself in Widow, much as she might like to. They had to do something—fast.

"Mags." Christie was gently stroking her friend's shorn head. "Lots of girls on the team have much shorter hair. We just have to get you to someone who can even this out. You might actually like it," Christie added in a desperate attempt to cheer Maggie up.

At the moment, Maggie looked like a mutt of vastly different parentage who has also been through both a hurricane and a tornado.

Maggie was sitting, slumped over, between them. Maybe I could wear a ski cap all winter, she thought dismally.

"Amber likes it. She thinks it's very 'hip,' very 'happening,' very me." Maggie's voice was dull and she repeated the words without much intonation.

Vicky felt herself getting mad again. "Why on earth did you let her cut your hair! Did she tell you she knew how?"

"Not exactly," Maggie admitted. The whole scene came back and she was feeling slightly ashamed of herself for being such a wimp. She'd stopped by Amber's room to drop off a book Amber had loaned her. Amber was there with some of her friends and they had invited Maggie to stay and have some coffee. Feeling flattered, Maggie sat down. They were talking about the dance and what they were going to wear, how they were going to do their hair. That's when Amber had made her suggestion: "Margaret, don't you think those long curls are . . . well, a little childish?" She drew the last word out and some of her friends snickered. Maggie felt about three years old. "Well, actually, I've been growing it out. Maybe it's a little longer in some parts," she stammered.

"I could trim it for you," Amber offered. "You'd look much more hip tonight. Much more happening."

Before she knew it, Maggie had a towel around her shoulders and Amber had scissors in her hand. At

74

the sound of the first snip, she'd changed her mind and said, "I think I'll make an appointment at Hair Stop and get it trimmed there. Maybe I can do it this afternoon."

"Too late," Amber said mockingly. "Don't be such a coward. Women who dare to take up the pen can't get upset over a few fallen tresses." And that's when Maggie had wimped out.

The other girls suddenly vanished and Maggie sat in agony as clump after clump of hair fell to the ground. At one point, Amber said peevishly, "It just doesn't want to get even." Finally, she declared it a masterpiece and allowed Maggie to look in the mirror. Maggie had managed not to cry until she was outside the dorm.

Now Vicky said firmly, after Maggie had related her tale of woe, "Going to Hair Stop is a great idea. We'll tell them it's an emergency. Put a hat or something on and let's get out of here. Afterwards, we'll think what to do to get back at Amber."

"Get back at Amber?" Maggie asked, "What do you mean? You don't believe she did this on purpose, do you?"

Christie shook her head in disbelief. Did Maggie's balloon ever land? "Let's get your hair fixed and then talk. But think about it—would you cut someone's hair, especially if she seemed reluctant?"

"Well, no, yet why would she want to make me look ugly?"

"Who knows? Maybe she's jealous," Christie offered.

"Now, that is *crazy*," Maggie insisted. "I'm the last person in the world Amber St. James would ever want to be like."

With Maggie's hair the way it looked now, Vicky was forced to agree, but Maggie on a good hair day— she could run rings around the tenth grader.

"Mon Dieu!" Monsieur Paul cried when Maggie took off her hat. Then he added, *"Quelle horreur,"* thus causing Vicky to doubt her previous notion that the man's French accent had originated in Brooklyn.

He quickly collected himself and set to work, the light of challenge in his eye. While the other two girls read their way through a stack of *People* magazines, he clipped and coaxed Maggie's hair into something that was not just passable but great.

"Wow!" Vicky exclaimed. "You look terrific!" Maggie smiled shyly. Her hair was definitely short, but she liked it. The two sides were still uneven, yet now it seemed done on purpose, one brushing her chin, the other tucked behind her ear. Monsieur Paul had thinned the bangs and parted them—"to emphasize those *magnifique* eyes and *chic* glasses," he said. Her oversized red frames *did* look more fashionable, Maggie thought. He trimmed the back to match the chin-length side, letting her natural wave give body to the cut.

Christie giggled, then guffawed. "What's so funny?" Maggie asked, a sudden pang of doubt hitting her.

"Oh Maggie, I can't wait to see the look on Amber's face when she sees 'her' haircut!"

"Come on," Vicky said, grabbing her friend's arm. "We have to go find something for Cinderella to wear to the ball."

Monsieur Paul bowed. The girls told him he was a genius. He watched them leave, an affectionate look on his face, before turning to one of the other stylists with a scowl. "I'd like to get my hands on the little witch that did that to her," he said angrily—and without a trace of an accent.

The gym at Mansfield Hill had not exactly been transformed into a palace, but with some streamers, slightly lowered lights, and plenty of loud music, it no longer resembled the place where a few hours earlier hordes of sweaty boys had chased one another from one basketball hoop to the other.

Trust was a big thing at both schools. It had been the focal point of the eighth-grade Outward Bound trip the previous fall, and teachers talked about it so frequently that Vicky commented to her roommates how she often felt she was at some sort of bank instead of a school: "You know, The Cabot Trust Company." Both Cabot and Mansfield assumed you would not break the rules, so the doors to the outside were open—"Thank goodness for the air," Christie said gratefully when she noticed them—but you weren't supposed to go through.

Maggie was feeling weird. Her shoulders felt bare, even though she was wearing a black tank top under an oversized denim shirt, both Vicky's. She kept reaching for her hair—and she was looking for

Amber, she told Vicky, who was by her side drinking punch. Christie was dancing with Scott.

"I'm looking for her, too," Vicky said emphatically. "She's probably way too cool to come to a high school dance, though. Not when she can hang out with college kids."

"You really don't like her, do you?" Maggie asked bluntly, wondering why she hadn't picked up on it before. It was hard to defend Amber's cutting her hair, but after all, Maggie hadn't really protested very hard. "If you only got to know her better—"

Vicky cut her off, "Look, Mags, any friend of yours is a friend of mine, but it's true that I think we probably don't have a lot in common." Like taking advantage of people, Vicky thought, fuming silently.

"Well, maybe we could invite her over sometime or—wait, there she is!"

Amber St. James and her Mansfield/Cabot friends had entered the gym. Even though it was crowded, they still managed to create a stir. One boy had dyed his hair bright orange for the event, and although black was still the color of choice, most of them had accentuated their outfits with various accessories. Amber wore a necklace that seemed to consist of a broken wineglass suspended from a rusty wire hanger.

"Let her find you," Vicky hissed. Above all, she didn't want her roommate to go galloping across the floor to be humiliated in some way by this group. Let Amber find out for herself how Maggie's coiffure looked now.

Maggie fidgeted. Yet she knew Vicky was right somehow. She just hadn't figured out why yet.

With Amber located, Vicky could turn her full attention to what she considered a much more important task—finding Mrs. Babcox and telling her about Blair. Maggie's catastrophe had taken center stage, but it was time to get back to Blair. The headmistress was nowhere in sight—and neither, of course, was Blair. They'd talked about the dance earlier in the week and the girls had urged Blair to come. They could get permission from the housemother for her to stay over. Blair had seemed excited—before she disappeared.

Music filled the air. Scott and Christie had stopped dancing before the next song started. Now they were sitting on the floor, a plate with several pizza slices between them, talking about diving, of course.

Christie knew that Scott loved the sport as much as she did, but he also was depending on it to help him get a college scholarship. He was the oldest of five children, and although both his parents worked, there wasn't enough money to pay for college for everyone. He was on a scholarship at Mansfield and worked hard to keep his grades up.

Christie thought he was under a lot of pressure for someone his age and now the words flew out of her mouth. This sometimes happened to her. It was like diving: You just went off the platform or the board without thinking too much.

"You're under so much pressure. I mean, all the

work at school, the team, and your job." Scott worked as a library aide.

"Yeah, sometimes I do feel like I want to blow my stack. No, that's not right. That I want to have a whole day with nothing to do except maybe practice. But then I know that I have to keep doing all these things if I'm ever going to be what I want."

Christie sighed. Scott was another one of those people with a firm goal. He wanted to be a doctor, specializing in sports medicine. Sometimes she felt the whole world knew what and where they would be in the next century except her.

"What's the matter?" Scott was quick to pick up on Christie's moods. He knew all about her mother, and they'd been able, after a long while, to talk a bit about it.

"You, and my friends. You all seem to know just what you want. I haven't got a clue." That reminded her of Blair, and, changing the subject, she quickly told Scott about their worries.

"Why don't we walk around and see if we can spot Mrs. Babcox?" he suggested. They got up and disposed of the empty plate.

"And," he added, "don't think you're the only one who hasn't decided every minute of his or her future. I have plenty of doubts about mine, and I'm sure your friends do, too. I mean, how can we possibly know at our age how things are going to turn out? I think you're smarter than the rest of us, and maybe more honest. Half the time, I say I want to be a doctor 'cause it keeps people off my back. Most adults are always at you with the big old 'what do you want to be?' question."

He reached for Christie's hand.

Mrs. Babcox was still nowhere to be seen, but Amber had spotted Maggie. As she did so, her mouth opened wide. She started to walk over, then turned abruptly around and headed for the refreshments.

"I wouldn't have pegged Amber as a pizza lover," Vicky remarked snidely. "More eye of newt—oops, sorry, Mags." She had resolved to keep her Amber St. James opinions from her roommate, but it had slipped out. Maggie didn't seem to have heard the remark. She was still staring after Amber and her entourage. Just then, Mark Reese came over.

"Hi, Vicky. Want to dance?"

Vicky looked at Maggie. She really wanted to dance with Mark, but she didn't want to leave her friend stranded. Again, Maggie was off in her own world and didn't even notice Mark standing in front of them.

"I'm going to get something to eat," Maggie said. "Oh, hi, Mark. How's it going?"

"Fine. Well then . . ." He reached for Vicky's hand. Something was going on and he was bound to find out. Vicky Lee was not only extremely pleasant to look at but she also managed to get herself involved in all sorts of real-life dramas. They walked over to where everyone was dancing and passed Amber's group, sitting in a dark heap on the bleachers. Several of them greeted Mark and he raised a hand in reply.

"I'm way too sexy for my grade," he said, mimicking the commercial, and Vicky laughed. "Plus, they're so far above our little mundane Drama Club or the literary magazine. The truth is, they'd end up painting scenery and getting their stuff rejected. Not that this doesn't happen to the rest of us, but God forbid they should even give this place a try."

Vicky was surprised at how bitter Mark sounded. He was president of his class and very easygoing. The combination of his even temperament and high level of energy—a combination so much like her own—was what had attracted her to him. That and his voice! His performance as John Proctor in the play had been riveting.

"You never talk this way. Do you know something about these kids I don't? Because if you do, I need to find out."

"Oh, you 'need to find out' everything, Ms. Marple. But yeah, I have a very good reason for not liking those particular kids—besides the fact that they're a bunch of phonies. They get their kicks picking on other kids. Last year, they scapegoated a new boy in our class. He had a slight stutter and was from someplace in the Midwest. His dad got transferred to the Boston area and he ended up here. Anyway, they used to rag on him all the time, and if some other kids and one of the teachers hadn't picked up on it, I don't know what Tim might have done."

"Tim! You mean Reverend Hale?" Vicky was astonished. He'd been cast as the minister in the play and had been fantastic.

"Yeah, it's weird. When he's acting, the stutter goes away. He didn't want anyone to do anything about the situation, but it really ticked me off. Word got out, and he's ended up being one of the most popular kids in our class, which these aliens"—he gestured toward the bleachers—"are not. I heard a rumor this afternoon that the girls in the group shaved some poor girl's head today. That's sick."

Vicky told him the whole story. Mark had helped Christie & Company solve the mystery last fall, and now she was glad to have him as a strong ally in Amber's comeuppance—or, more precisely, downfall. And down she would fall. Vicky and Christie would see to that.

She was just about to start hatching various plans with Mark when she spotted Mrs. Babcox entering the gym.

"Gotta go. I'll catch you later. I have to see Mrs. Babcox!" Vicky sped off, calling back, "I'll explain everything."

A *very* interesting girl, thought Mark.

"So, you see, we've been very worried about her." Vicky had tackled Mrs. Babcox before the woman even had a chance to take her coat off. She looked at the extremely earnest eighth grader in front of her, paused to give her coat to a student who came to hang it up for her, and suggested that Vicky accompany her out into the hall. It wasn't happy news.

"I'm afraid Blair underestimated the workload

here. She was feeling overwhelmed and has decided to go back to her old school in Boston."

"But she was so happy at Cabot! It was her dream to come here, even when she was living in Taiwan!" Vicky protested.

"I know. Blair Samuels wrote to me often about her delightful English student, but Mrs. Chan was very definite. She felt Blair's health might suffer. Apparently, she was staying up very late to do her homework."

"She didn't seem tired. Maybe she was just coming down with something." Vicky still couldn't believe the news.

"I told her Blair could reapply for next year. Maybe she needs more time to find her feet in a new country, especially after losing her father. I'm grateful to you and your friends for watching out for Blair. I'm sure she'll want to hear from you."

Glumly, Vicky said, "We don't even have her phone number."

"Fortunately, I do." Mrs. Babcox put her arm around Vicky's shoulders. "You can get it from Mrs. Watson on Monday. Now, let's go back to the dance and have some fun."

It wasn't until Vicky was climbing the bleachers to where Maggie, Christie, Scott, Mark, and some other kids were sitting that she remembered.

Remembered that Mrs. Chan didn't speak any English.

🐉 Chapter Seven

"**S**o it couldn't have been her mother on the phone!" Vicky had just finished telling the others about her conversation with Mrs. Babcox.

"Then who was it? Blair?" asked Scott.

"It must have been," Christie answered, "but why would she leave Cabot, especially without telling us, or at least Vicky?"

This was what had been bothering Vicky, too. She had thought she and Blair were good friends. No, she *knew* they were. Something was terribly, terribly wrong.

"And she wasn't falling behind," Maggie added. "She got an *A* on the science quiz, and it was really tough. In fact, she offered to help me with some of the things I didn't get. She loved the work here. Remember the joke she made at lunch—that she felt like a sponge that had been in the sun too long finally dropped in a pail of water!"

"The only problem she seemed to have was getting lost," Vicky explained to the boys. "If there had been anything else, she'd have said something. I'm sure!"

"Okay," said Mark, "you're the detectives. If she didn't drop out of Cabot because of the work, why did she? And why did she pretend to be her mother?"

"The last part's easy," Christie said immediately, and her roommates nodded. "Obviously, she couldn't call up the headmistress and say she was leaving herself. She had to pretend to be an adult in order to make it all official. Besides, she's probably so used to speaking for her mother that she doesn't even think of it as pretending."

"And there's the whole face-saving thing," Vicky quickly added. "Blair wouldn't want the school to know her mother doesn't speak English. I'm sure her mother agrees."

"That answers the second question: what about the first?" Mark persisted.

Christie & Company looked at one another.

They were stumped.

"Maybe—" Maggie said. But whatever else she was going to say got cut off by Vicky's cry.

"My Dad is here! I've got to run. I had no idea it was so late, and I said I'd be at the door waiting for him. Oh dear, he looks completely lost!" She ran down the bleachers and over to her father, who was indeed looking around the gym with the bewildered air of someone who finds himself in a very foreign country—or, more precisely, distant planet.

Maggie explained Vicky's sudden departure to the group. "This weekend is the Chinese New Year, or rather the beginning of it, and Vicky has to help get ready. She told us that even though her mother and grandmother have been cleaning the house for weeks, they still need her early tomorrow to make sure everything is perfect. You're supposed to start the year with a clean slate—all your debts paid, arguments settled, and wearing a new outfit, so the evil spirits won't recognize you."

"Well, Vicky won't protest about that last tradition." Mark laughed. Vicky had told him about the New Year's customs and he had been very interested in them. He, Scott, and some other guys from Mansfield planned to go to the festivities in Boston's Chinatown on Sunday. It was the beginning of the Year of the Dragon, Vicky had told him, the luckiest year of all in the Chinese lunar calendar. Pregnant women about to deliver were desperately hoping their little bundles of joy would hold off a few days and enter the world with this extra dose of good luck. Vicky had said she agreed—she certainly would rather be born in the Year of the Dragon than the Year of the Rabbit, the year ending now!

"I was born in the Year of the Boar, or the Pig," she'd told him. "That's very lucky, too, especially if you have a restaurant, because the pig stands for wealth. People born in the Year of the Pig are supposed to be very honest, have many friends, accomplish what they set out to do—and be very stubborn. My mother brings that one up a lot!"

Mark had asked to find out which of the twelve animals in the calendar was his birth sign, and she had promised to figure it out. He made a mental note to remind her. Maybe he was a dragon!

Maggie stretched her legs out onto the riser below. She'd had several compliments on her hair and the day was ending much better than she'd thought it would, except for the gnawing worry about Blair. Amber and her friends seemed to have left the gym. A pizza dance probably wasn't their idea of fun. No coffee, for one thing. Now where did that come from? If Amber liked coffee, and, she'd told Maggie—rather, Margaret—an occasional cigar, "the thin ones," that was her business. All Maggie knew was that Amber truly appreciated her as a writer. It was one thing for Vicky and Christie to say her stuff was good. They were her best friends. But Amber was totally objective. Wasn't she?

Christie and Maggie had been invited to the New Year's banquet the Lees were giving on Sunday at The Ginger Jar for their employees, friends, and relatives. Before that, the three girls planned to go to Chinatown to see the Lion Dances. It was going to be great. Maggie planned to spend tomorrow getting all her homework done. There *was* a lot of work, but it wasn't too much. Maggie thought about Blair again. Something was wrong with the whole story.

"She's simply disappeared into thin air, I'm afraid. There's nothing we can do without a scrap of evidence to go on. We've come to the end of our rope. There is one chance, though. . . ."

"What is it? We'll do anything!" the headmistress said breathlessly. "Please, Chief MacIsaac, tell me. What can we do? We have to find the girl!"

"She doesn't take many cases, but she just might take this one. You probably remember the Creve, Lump and Rowe jewelry store robbery a few years back. Well, she cracked that one."

"Who is it? We must engage her, no matter what the cost!"

"Nobody knows her real name. She's listed in the directory as Margaret Marple, Inc."

The harried headmistress was already leafing through the Yellow Pages.

An hour later, the girl was back safe and sound. "Piece of cake," the detective told the astonished Aleford police chief, "and make that moon cake."

"Maggie, Maggie, wherever you are." A Mansfield eighth grader, nicknamed "Ludwig" for his musical ability, was tugging at her denim sleeve. "Come back to the land of the living and dance with me!"

At home in Brookline, Vicky wasn't sleeping well. She was worried about Blair. At about six o'clock, she heard a noise in the apartment. Her parents got up early, but not this early. Who was stirring? Maybe her grandmother was having a cup of tea. The old lady didn't sleep very much, claiming she didn't need as much time to dream as she used to.

Not wanting to startle her grandmother, Vicky tiptoed out of her room and crept down the hall, where she was startled in turn! Grandmother was completely dressed. Her coat was on the chair by the door to the apartment. Where on earth could she be going at this time of day? Or any time of day? Mrs. Lee did not venture out of the apartment alone, even to go to the restaurant, a short trolley ride away.

Quickly, Vicky padded silently back to her room and threw on some clothes. When she got to the door, her grandmother *and* her coat were gone. Vicky grabbed her own things from the closet and ran down the stairs. Her grandmother would have taken the elevator. Was someone meeting her outside? She did play mah-jong with a group of ladies every week and was picked up for that. Was there some special New Year's game starting at dawn?

But when she got to the sidewalk in front of her house, the only cars were parked ones. She looked down Beacon Street and was just in time to see her grandmother disappear around the corner. The old woman was walking briskly. Vicky was excited. Maybe this was the secret of the roses blooming in Mrs. Lee's cheeks. Maybe her grandmother had taken up walking! But in this weather? Much of the snow had been melted by last week's sun, but more winter was surely on the way. It wasn't even February yet.

The simplest thing would have been to catch up to Mrs. Lee and ask her what she was doing, but Vicky found herself reluctant to confront her grandmother. Obviously, this was something Mrs. Lee wanted to keep to herself. Yet Vicky had to find out! So she followed at a distance. It wasn't hard to shadow the small figure, bundled up in a bright blue quilted jacket and cap, through the empty early-morning street. At one of the stoplights, Vicky was surprised to see another similar figure join her grandmother. Then a block later, two more women greeted them and they all walked on together. Was it some sort of club?

Finally, they entered a large building. Vicky climbed the stairs, afraid to let them out of her sight, but she was so surprised when she pushed open the doors and discovered a large sign welcoming her to the Jewish Community Center that she lost track of them. Grandmother attended church in Chinatown and was also a firm follower of Confucius, the ancient Chinese scholar. She had taught Vicky his most famous saying at a very early age: "What you do not want done to yourself, do not do to others." Why would her grandmother be coming here?

Cautiously, Vicky went down the corridor and stood there listening for sounds of activity. She didn't hear a thing. At the end, there were two large double doors. She was about to turn around and explore the rest of the building when she heard a cough. She pushed one door open slightly and peered in. The sight that greeted her eyes was so amazing, she had to clamp her hand over her mouth to keep from crying out.

About forty women, all Asian and all her grandmother's age, were silently standing in rows, vigorously rotating their arms over their heads. As she watched, they suddenly squatted close to the floor and struck the ground with their hands. Vicky was about to close the door and leave, her grandmother's secret safe, when one of the women saw her and called out in Chinese, "Do not be shy, little one. Come join us!"

Vicky was mortified. All eyes were upon her. She stood still. Would her grandmother ever forgive her for embarrassing her in front of her friends?

"It is my granddaughter, Vicky. The one I have told you about. She is a very clever girl," Mrs. Lee told the group, the admiration in her voice plain. "I should have known she would find out what I was doing. My own son has not noticed at all!" The ladies giggled. Vicky let her breath out. Grandmother wasn't angry.

"I'm sorry for interrupting you. I was worried that something might be wrong. Except Grandmother looks so good. You all do!" Now it was Vicky's turn to express her admiration.

"Before doing *lok tong kuin,* my stomach was way out here," one woman said, gesturing. "Now see how flat it is!"

Vicky nodded and said, "Maybe I can join you another time, but I should go home. If my parents wake up and find both of us gone, they'll think we ran away or something!"

The women laughed and returned to their exercises. Mrs. Lee came over to Vicky and they went out into the corridor.

"I was too much in the apartment and I missed my little peacock. My friend told me about the group. In good weather, we meet in the park. The center lets us use this room when it's too cold or there's too much snow. I am usually home before your parents wake, or if not, I tell them I have been walking. It's fun to have a secret, and I have many new friends now, too.

"What is *lok tong kuin?*" Vicky asked. "Is it like *tai chi?*"

"Yes, plus some more exercises. We were doing the 'Windmill' first, then 'Hitting the Drum While Riding the Horse,' very good for getting the blood to your stomach. I will teach them to you and you can do them with Christie and Maggie. Now, hurry home and I will see you later." Her grandmother gave her a quick squeeze, a much firmer one than in the pre-calisthenics days.

Vicky found herself running home. The sight of all the ladies doing the "Windmill" kept going through her mind, and she was still smiling when she eased open the apartment door. Her parents were awake but assumed she wasn't. She slipped into her room, put her pajamas back on, and walked into the kitchen, sleepily rubbing her eyes. Grandmother's secret was safe with her. One mystery was solved. Now she had to get busy on the other one.

Christie & Company had made a pact early on—no going solo. They were a team. Accordingly, Vicky called the dorm and asked to speak to her roommates. It took awhile for them to get to the phone on the ground floor, but when they did, she outlined her plan to find out why Blair had left Cabot.

"I know we said no going out on our own, but in this case, I think we should make an exception. After I finish helping here, I want to go to Tai Tung Village, where the Chans live. I'm sure I'll be able to find their apartment. I don't want to wait until Monday to call Blair. If she's in trouble, she needs our help now. I plan to say I lost my friend's apartment number and ring a few doorbells."

Maggie and Christie were holding the phone so both could hear, and they started to speak simultaneously. "You go first," Maggie said, and Christie told Vicky, "This is a time that calls for your expertise. We don't speak Chinese, and it might make people less willing to talk if we were along. Go for it."

Maggie agreed. "Call us the minute you find anything out, and if what you find is Blair, tell her she's got to come back!"

Vicky hung up and set out for Chinatown. Her mother had decided that she needed another miniature tangerine tree, a traditional New Year's decoration, and some more *hong bao,* the small red envelopes decorated with symbols of good fortune that would hold the "lucky money" the Lees planned to distribute. Vicky would go to the Tai Tung apartment complex first, then do her mother's shopping.

Chinatown was bustling, the sidewalks crowded with shoppers getting ready for the New Year. Tai Tung was a short walk from Beach Street, the center of Chinatown. The door in the entry was open. Vicky scanned the mailboxes. As she had suspected, there were quite a few Chans. She wrote down some apartment numbers and slipped in the main door, which was locked, when someone was coming out.

No one was home at the first Chan apartment or

the second. At the third, she got lucky. A woman about her mother's age answered the door and, after hearing Vicky's story, invited her in.

"I know everyone here. Now tell me your friend's name."

"It's Chan, Bì Yún Chan. I don't know her mother's name. Her father died last August, but she has a baby brother, Meǐ Shēng."

The woman looked puzzled. "There is no one living here with those names."

Vicky felt a cold stab of fear. "They arrived from Taiwan a year ago last November, Mrs. Chan and Bì Yún, I mean. Mr. Chan was already living here, and Meǐ Shēng wasn't born yet."

"There is an eight-year wait to get into these apartments," the woman told Vicky sorrowfully. She could feel the girl's anxiety. "A man alone would not be occupying an apartment large enough for a family. I think you must have the wrong address."

Vicky thanked her and left. Instead of solving the mystery, she had added to it. Why had Blair wanted them to think she lived at Tai Tung? Vicky remembered seeing Blair leave the building immediately after they had dropped her off that night. It hadn't been her home. But where did she really live, and how was Vicky ever going to find her?

And why had Blair wanted them to believe she lived somewhere she didn't? Vicky looked at her watch. She had to hurry to the stores and do her mother's errands. She didn't want to start the New Year with a quarrel. It would be very bad luck.

Struggling with the large plant, after having tucked the red envelopes safely in the pocket of her jacket, Vicky made her way back to the subway. The sidewalks were still filled with people, jostling one another good-naturedly as they struggled with their bundles. Many carried plants like Vicky's. Suddenly in the sea of faces, she saw her friend. It was Blair!

Vicky shouted her name, but the girl was too far ahead to hear. Her head was ducked down and she was moving rapidly. Vicky followed as fast as she could. First her grandmother, now Blair. The coincidence of trailing two people in one day would have been comical if the situation was less serious. Blair turned down an alley and disappeared into a dilapidated apartment building wedged between a small Asian grocery store and a factory building. Vicky was about to follow, then realized she didn't have time. It was getting dark, as well. Almost New Year's Eve. She noted the number of the building. She'd be back early the next morning—with Christie & Company in full force.

Blair Chan trudged wearily up the dark stairs. There were no lights, except what filtered in from the street through the filthy windows. The landlord had never repaired the fixtures. Her eyes were filled with tears. She blinked them away. She did not want to worry her mother, especially now. She thought of her father. I'm doing the best I can, she told him silently. He would have been very upset at where they were living, but that had happened right after he died. There was very little money and the rent had been more than they could afford. It would only be for a little while, her mother had said, until the life-insurance money came. Mr. Chan had prudently provided for them, paying a friend who was in the business each month.

Well, the money had finally come, but look what had happened! Blair felt the tears again, then anger. She passed the toilet they shared with the whole floor, a floor of strangers. It symbolized everything she hated about the place. You had to hold your breath and use it quickly. Cabot had been a haven. The showers at the gym were a luxury she'd never known.

She unlocked the door and forced herself to greet her mother cheerfully. *"Gōng xi fa cai!"* It was the New Year's greeting she'd heard echoing on the streets below—"Happiness and fortune to you!"

Her mother was putting on her coat to go to work. The two of them went and looked at Mason. Mrs. Chan kissed her daughter's face and stroked the soundly sleeping baby's hair.

"Good not to know, little boy. Sleep well," she whispered.

Chapter Eight

Chinatown was quiet on Sunday morning. The streets were covered with red paper confetti from the strings of firecrackers set off all during the noisy night as celebrants marked the return of the Kitchen God to earth. He'd been away all week on his long journey to the Palace of the Jade Emperor high in the sky, where he'd made his report on the good and bad deeds of each family below.

The smell of smoke still hung in the air. It was cold and the sky was overcast, but most of the snow was gone. A few piles, blackened by exhaust and dirt, had been left by the plows—stubborn reminders of previous storms. Vicky shivered and said to her roommates, who were standing by her side, "Not a very pretty New Year's Day. In a way, I hope it does snow and cover up all this mess, at least for a little while."

Christie and Maggie had been given permission to spend the previous night at Christie's house. Mr. Montgomery was delighted to see his daughter and her friend again so soon, but he also sensed something was up. Christie told him about Blair and that they wanted to see if she was all right. What she didn't mention was Vicky's anxious call telling them about her experience at the apartment complex and urging the girls to meet her as early as possible in Chinatown the next morning.

Now they were gathered at the end of the alley where the Chans' apartment was located.

"Do you think it's too early?" Maggie asked. "Maybe they're still sleeping." It was only seven o'clock.

"No one will be able to sleep much longer. The celebrating has only stopped for a little while. It's why I wanted to get here now."

The girls entered the building. None of them had ever been in such a place. There was no lock on the front door and all the mailboxes had been pried open. Newspapers littered the floor and there was a smell of rancid cooking oil and something else that caused Maggie to cough. It was clear to all of them why Blair hadn't wanted them to know where she lived.

They went up the first flight and Vicky quickly looked at the names taped on the doors. No Chans.

On the top floor, two of the doors didn't have names.

"It has to be one of these," Christie said softly. "All the other doors have names. Which one? We have a fifty-fifty chance."

Maggie thought about a short story her writing class had read recently. It was about a man also facing two closed doors. Behind one was a lady; behind the other, a tiger. This felt the same—the lady or the tiger? She closed her eyes and pointed, but they didn't need to guess after all. A baby's insistent cry came from behind one of the flimsy wood panels. He wanted food and he wanted some now, the cry seemed to say. It stopped almost immediately. Someone had picked him up.

"Mason," Vicky declared, and knocked at the door.

No one answered, and she sensed that all movement in the apartment had ceased.

She knocked again and called out in Chinese, "Bì Yún, it's me, Vicky."

The door opened immediately, yet Blair's face was not covered by her usual broad smile. It was filled with fear.

"Vicky—Christie, Maggie. What are you doing here? You cannot stay! You must go quickly!"

"Blair!" Vicky pleaded. "We know something is wrong. Maybe we can help. Please tell us what's going on!"

The baby in her arms began to cry again and Blair seemed unsure what to do.

"I have to take care of my brother. My mother is . . . out."

Again Vicky tried to convince the girl. "You are in trouble. I can tell. You *have* to let us do what we can."

Blair's eyes filled with tears and she motioned them into the room. She picked up a bottle and gave it to Mason. He sucked greedily, his plump little cheeks turning red with the exertion.

"He's adorable!" Christie exclaimed, diverted for a moment by the sight of the happy baby. "Do you think he would let me hold him?"

Blair did smile then. "Oh yes, he is very friendly." Then she sighed. "I am sorry not to welcome you to a nicer home."

The room was tiny. There was a hot plate for cooking, a bed, a table, and three chairs, but no phone. Stacks of boxes and a chest of drawers completed the furnishings. Vicky noticed there were no New Year's decorations, not even the "Spring Couplets," poems on strips of red paper hung on the doorway in Chinese homes at this time of year. New Year's was also called the Spring Festival—spring, the time of new beginnings. The only sign of the season was a plate with three very old-looking oranges on it and the remains of some incense. The Chans had been honoring their ancestors and departed loved ones last night. Vicky thought of the mounds of juicy oranges and apples at the restaurant and her home, plus all the other symbols of good luck the Lees had spread throughout the restaurant and their apartment. She felt guilty for having so much.

"Nobody cares," Christie said, reassuring Blair about the room. She took little Mason, who did indeed snuggle comfortably in her arms, and sat down on one of the chairs. "Now tell us why you left and everything you've been leaving out of what Maggie calls 'the story.'"

The directness worked and Blair sat down on the floor, motioning the others to the chairs, but Maggie and Vicky promptly joined her. She hesitated only for a moment, then started to speak.

"We are in very serious trouble. I have tried to convince my mother to go to the police or at least one of the agencies here that help people, but she is very frightened and I cannot reason with her. It would be different if she spoke English, or we were citizens, or, of course, if my father were alive. But none of these things is true.

"Last Tuesday night, three men came to the apartment. I was doing my homework, my mother was sewing, and Mason was in his little seat. We were not frightened at first, because one of the men was my father's friend. He was the one who had sold my father his life insurance, and my mother has been asking him and asking him when it would come, so we could move. Except he was not a friend. He is an enemy. He told my mother that the insurance check would be coming but that my father owed money to the other two men for our passage to this country. The insurance check would not be enough to pay the debt, but it would be a start."

"How much could it have been!" Christie exclaimed. "Life insurance is usually a great deal of money."

"We were supposed to get forty thousand dollars. My father explained everything to us and made us hide the papers in a secret place to keep them safe. But the men said he owed them fifty thousand dollars for our passages and papers. They also told my mother that her marriage to my father was not legal in this country and she could be deported. They said because the marriage was illegal, Mason would not be recognized as a citizen of the United States!" Blair began to sob. The strain of the last days finally caused her to break down.

"But this is all wrong!" Vicky exploded. "Did they have anything in writing signed by your father?" She knew that Blair was not exaggerating the prices people paid to come to this country, yet Mr. Chan would not have needed to do that to bring his wife and child over when he was a legal immigrant gainfully employed, who had obtained citizenship.

"They waved some papers but would not let us see them closely. They were shouting at my mother, and she does not know whether to believe them or not. All she can think of is how to stay here and get the money to pay them. We had to take Mason out of his day care. It was too expensive. And my mother has taken a job in a restaurant, besides the sewing. I am studying at home for now to watch my brother; otherwise, we will have to send him to my grandmother in Taiwan so she can take care of him. We might never see him again! We can't let him go!"

"Of course not," Maggie said, "But what you need is a lawyer, and maybe the police."

"My father is a lawyer and I know he'll help," Christie said excitedly. "Everything will be fine, you'll see."

Blair shook her head sadly. "I don't think so. Now I understand that my mother has been worried for a long time about this money. She has been uneasy about this 'friend,' yet she did not tell me. I knew she was keeping something back, but I thought it was about work. They have been cheating her there, too.

"The men came back again Thursday night. They said the check would go to the bank where our account is the next day, and they ordered my mother to collect the cash. We are supposed to put it in a knapsack and turn it over to another man who will be waiting with them at the corner of Tyler and Beach Streets today at two o'clock."

"Why did they want to wait until today? Why didn't they take it Friday night?" Vicky wondered out loud.

"I don't know," Blair said. "My mother and I have been over and over it. When they left, I listened at the door, because I heard them talking in the hall. They said something about someone from New York. Maybe he is the leader and does not trust them to do this themselves."

This was serious, Vicky thought to herself. Her cousin Teddy had told her about the increase in gang activity in Boston's Chinatown by gangs from New York seeking to broaden their territory. The Chans had gotten caught in the web. The gang members were no doubt counting on the confusion of the Lion Dances and firecrackers to cover this pickup and maybe others.

"You're sure your mother won't go to the police?" she asked Blair.

"I'm sure. The men told us not to tell anyone or try to get away; otherwise, it would be very bad for us." She had been certain they were carrying weapons. When they made the threat, one man smiled an evil smile and patted his jacket pocket. He was clearly enjoying their fear.

Mason was using Christie as a jungle gym, pulling himself up and babbling delightedly. The contrast between the cheerful baby and the threat that hung in the stale apartment air was enormous.

For once, Maggie found herself with nothing to say. What *could* they do?

Christie wished Blair would let her tell Mr. Montgomery, who would know which authorities to inform, but she understood Mrs. Chan's fears. She cast about for other alternatives.

But it was Vicky who came up with the solution.

"Did you ever see a movie called *The Sting?*" she asked.

The biggest problem was convincing Teddy.

"No thank you, little cousin. This is way too dangerous, and I would like to keep on speaking, and eating, terms with my aunt and uncle." The three girls had gone to Winthrop House at Harvard and dragged him out of bed. He'd been celebrating the New Year with his family the night before, telling stories and eating until the wee hours. He'd planned to sleep until it was almost time for the banquet at The Ginger Jar.

"There's absolutely no risk to us. We *have* to have your help. The police are not going to go along with the plan of three eighth graders; we need you to tell them. Come on, Teddy, we can't just stand by and let these guys take the Chans' money. There's no way Mrs. Chan can support them, and Blair deserves a chance at Cabot. It's not fair!"

Teddy looked at his cousin. How did she get herself—and him—into these things?

"All right, tell me the plan again. But first, one of you go downstairs and get me some coffee from the dining hall."

Maggie offered to go. Coffee seemed to be playing a major role in her life lately.

As the door closed, Vicky pushed some of her cousin's clothes from a chair and sat down. Christie perched on the arm.

"It's simple, practically foolproof. Blair is going to be waiting at the corner. She'll be wearing a blue cap with CABOT on the front in gold letters. Christie has one at home from the diving team. Just in case the police don't spot that, she'll be carrying a bunch of peacock feathers—I've got those. Of course, she'll also have the knapsack. When they approach her, she'll stall, cry a little, and they're bound to unzip it to make sure the money's inside and it's not just filled with lettuce leaves." For Christie's benefit she added, "The Chinese word for lettuce sounds like the word for money and treasure, so we always have plenty around at New Year's."

"That should give the police, who will have been instructed by you, plenty of time to move in and make the arrests," Christie finished.

"And where will you three be during all this? Safely in Brookline, I hope," Teddy added.

"And miss everything? Besides, it's our idea, and most important, we can't let Blair be alone. We'll be standing on the other side of the street, simply innocent visitors coming to watch the Lion Dances."

Maggie returned with Teddy's coffee. "Will he do it?"

Teddy took a sip. She'd put in much too much sugar.

"He'll do it," he said.

Blair was nervous. She had never gone against her mother's wishes before, but she felt that she was listening to her father's voice now. It was telling her she had to try to save the family.

Waiting until it was time to leave the apartment, the minutes seemed to drag by. It had not been easy to convince her mother, who had returned from one job, to let Blair be the one to take the knapsack to the corner. She finally succeeded by pointing out that the men might say something in English that could help the Chans later, assuming that Blair, like her mother, only spoke Chinese. This swayed her mother, who was also simply too tired to argue. Blair looked at her watch again. Not nearly time to leave. She was meeting the girls outside China Pearl at 1:30 to go over things once more.

As it turned out, the police were very interested in what Teddy Lee had to say. He had first called a friend from high school, Allen Woo, whose father was a detective. Detective Woo listened to Teddy and asked him to come to the station. "These people from New York are causing a lot of trouble in our neighborhood," he said. "This could be the opening we've been looking for." He listed to Christie & Company's plan, added some details, and sat down to wait himself. One of the conditions had been that he not get in touch with Mrs. Chan. The girls didn't even want Teddy to reveal Blair or her mother's name. They were afraid she would panic and not go along with the plan; plus, Blair was also insistent on it. Detective Woo understood the fears of newly arrived immigrants like Mrs. Chan. It was something the department was working on, adding more Chinese-speaking officers, especially those who were fluent in many dialects. With the control of Hong Kong reverting back to the People's Republic, many more newcomers had arrived.

Armed with cap and peacock feathers, Christie & Company assembled in front of the China Pearl restaurant. Had it only been a week ago that they'd met there for dim sum?

Around them, Chinatown resembled a war zone. Strings of firecrackers exploded like artillery in the streets and from the roofs of surrounding buildings. The street was even more thickly carpeted with the red bits of paper. Two different kung fu organizations, who trained and sponsored the Lion Dances, were filling the air with the noise of their enormous drums.

Keyed up, Maggie felt even more adrenaline rush through her veins when she saw the first dancers come through the archway at the end of Beach Street.

"They practice the steps for months," Vicky told

them. "The lion must never stop. Inside the head are strings the lead dancer pulls to make the ears wiggle and eyes move. There's a switch to light up the eyes, too. It's hard to coordinate all the movements. They're very precise."

The lion swooped and swirled, his long silken mane held high. When the mask was raised, they could see the dancers' faces, red handkerchiefs tied across their noses and mouths to keep out the smoke from the firecrackers, their ears muffled to dim the noise.

Someone tossed a string of firecrackers onto the sidewalk next to where they were standing. Christie jumped and Vicky laughed. "It's to scare away the evil spirits, not you!"

The lion stopped at each business, performing for the red envelope the owner would place in its mouth. Some storekeepers made the dancers work hard for the lucky money, hiding the envelope in lettuce leaves. Offerings of food—bright oranges and apples—were placed at the lion's feet.

The sky was still gray and the smoke made it seem as though a dense fog had settled on the narrow streets, yet the bleak day made the rainbow colors of the lion seem brighter, the gold-and-red costumes of the dancers more intense. The kung fu clubs carried huge flags, their bright colors waving high above the tumult. The New Year was beginning. A lucky year—the Year of the Dragon!

"Oh no!" Christie wailed, "Look!"

Coming toward them were Scott, Mark, and some other kids from Mansfield Hill. "How are we going to get rid of them? They'll see Blair and want to know what's happening."

Maggie thought fast and started speaking once the boys were close enough. "Isn't this awesome! And we found Blair. Everything is fine. In fact, she's meeting us here; then we're all going over to the arch at the end of the street to watch. It's got the best view." She had no idea whether this was true, yet it sounded reasonable. "Could you save us some places? She's a little late."

Mark smiled at Vicky. "Maybe she's lost again. Sure, we can save places, but first we want to score some of those dumplings I've been hearing so much about. There's a bakery right over there." He pointed across the street. We'll meet you by the arch after that."

"Phew," said Vicky as the boys waved good-bye and left. "Good thinking, Mags."

It was quarter to two. The girls were getting increasingly nervous. Where was Blair? At the corner, Teddy was lounging against the side of a shop with roast ducks hanging in the window. There were no uniformed police, but Vicky had the feeling that the man reading the newspaper not far from Teddy wasn't really reading. Of course, he could be one of the bad guys, too!

Blair appeared breathlessly, grabbed the cap and feathers, and said, "At the last minute, my mother changed her mind and wouldn't let me go. Finally, I just took the bag and ran. I had to." The girl was upset and dashed to the other side of the street. Her bright, shiny red Hello Kitty knapsack was easy to spot in the midst of the crowd. It had been a gift from her father when she'd first arrived in this country, she'd told the girls when she'd arrived at Cabot. Even though it certainly stood out from the somber Jan-Sport sacks most kids carried, Blair hadn't cared. It was a reminder of him.

Christie & Company watched her. "What if it doesn't work?" Maggie said dismally. The noise of the firecrackers was beginning to get on her nerves. It sounded too much like gunshots.

"It'll work. It has to," Vicky said fiercely.

When it happened, it happened so quickly, so chaotically, that afterward even those standing closest were not sure what they saw.

At two o'clock sharp, four men surrounded Blair. She cried and started to beg them to let her keep the money, but as soon as one man unzipped the knapsack, the plainclothes police moved in. At the same time, as they were leaving the bakery, the boys from Mansfield Hill saw Blair crying, assumed she was in trouble, and went rushing over, nearly tripping the Lion Dancers while dodging a ferocious barrage of firecrackers. The police, caught in the confusion of the New Year's revelers and would-be helpers, were unable to sort out who was who for a brief moment, and in that instant, the man with the knapsack escaped.

Christie & Company, poised on the opposite side of the street, could barely see because of the smoke.

"What's happening! Have they got them?" Christie yelled to Vicky, who was trying to push past the crowd and get across.

"Look!" screamed Maggie, pointed to a fleeing figure. "He's got Blair's knapsack!"

Without thinking, the three girls rushed across the parking lot after the man, who was carrying Blair's distinctive red Hello Kitty bag—the knapsack containing forty thousand dollars in cash.

He ducked into an alleyway and jumped into a pickup truck, with the back enclosed in plywood, the kind inexpensive restaurants use to transport food, and sometimes workers. The girls ran straight after him, but he was already in the driver's seat. They started to leap out of the way, expecting him to back up, when they realized two things; he'd flooded the engine and the door of the makeshift enclosure was ajar, right in front of their noses. Vicky slowly opened it a crack. Just as she had thought: There was no way to get to the cab of the truck from the rear, and no window. It was like a separate container and was in fact filled with sacks of rice and crates of groceries stacked high.

Christie and Vicky had barely managed to get in, pulling Maggie after them, when he finally got the truck started, reversed and, with tires squealing, sped off—where?

🐉 Chapter Nine

Maggie pushed the door handle down until it clicked into place. It wasn't too secure. The truck was moving rapidly, bouncing along as the driver seemed to hit every pothole in Boston.

The girls looked at one another, wide-eyed. What had they done? No risk, foolproof, Vicky had said to Teddy, but here they were hiding in what was probably a stolen vehicle, with a criminal at the wheel—a criminal, who, if not armed, was certainly dangerous. Christie moved slightly closer to Vicky. All three were lying flat by the door, afraid he might notice any large shifting of weight in the flimsy truck bed. Light crept in through the cracks in the plywood and it was cold. Christie nodded toward the cab. The rear window had been replaced with a wooden sliding panel. There was a hasp for a padlock, but no lock on it now. Vicky followed her gaze, all the more certain that this particular truck wasn't just used to transport bok choy and restaurant workers. Under the cover of night, there may have been any number of people crammed in here, being taken to places where they would be lucky to see daylight. She shuddered.

"The engine is pretty loud," Christie whispered in Vicky's ear, "but I don't think we should count on his not hearing us. He could stall or something. And we've got to hide, in case he opens the back door or that panel."

Vicky nodded and repeated to Maggie what Christie had said. It was like playing "telephone," only this wasn't play.

Maggie raised her head and motioned for the other two to follow her. She crawled along from the door toward a pile of empty burlap rice sacks. They were huge, but not quite big enough to hide in; still, it would be better than nothing. She pulled a sack over her feet. It came above her waist. The others did the same. Then they covered the upper portion of their bodies with more and settled in among the other sacks of rice. Protective coloration, Maggie remembered from science class, and wished she could share the joke with her friends.

Christie hoped she wouldn't sneeze. The burlap and pieces of rice clinging to it were making her nose tickle. She wondered how the rest of Christie & Company was doing.

They lay still. Each girl noted that the bumpy potholes had given way to a smooth surface. The truck slowed down and almost stopped, then gathered speed again. A tollbooth. They were on a highway.

It was pandemonium in Detective Woo's office. Mr. Lee and his mother were shouting at Teddy. Blair,

Mrs. Chan, and Mason were all crying. The detective was barking orders into his phone, and Calvin Montgomery was trying to get a word in edgewise with Detective Woo. Mark Reese, Scott Franklin, and Mrs. Lee were the only ones not making noise.

Finally the detective hung up. "Would everyone please be quiet so I can tell you what the department is doing?" He repeated it in Chinese, and Mrs. Chan took a deep breath, stopped her sobs, and put a pacifier in Mason's mouth.

"We have officers searching every building in Chinatown and the surrounding area, every street. The three men we arrested are being questioned. The moment we have any news, we will get in touch with you. You're welcome to stay here, but it's not the most comfortable place in the world—or the largest."

This was an understatement. The walls were lime green, the paint peeling. A battered gunmetal gray desk, swivel chair plus two other chairs, and several file cabinets completed the decor. There was one window, looking out over a Dumpster.

"I deeply regret what has occurred." He looked at the parents in front of him with obvious concern.

"I think we can assume that our daughters saw the man escaping with their friend's money and decided to follow him," Mr. Montgomery was saying.

"But they knew he was dangerous. Would they do something so foolish?" Detective Woo asked. Blair was crying again. It was all her fault.

It was Scott Franklin who answered the detective: "You don't know Christie and Company, sir."

Vicky took off the bag covering her face and looked at her watch. It was only 3:30. She felt as if they'd been driving for hours. As she lay nestled in the rice, she'd tried to think of a plan. There was no way the three could get into the cab of the truck, and even if they could, they wouldn't be able to overpower him if he had a weapon. She was still a little stunned by what they had done. It had just seemed the natural thing to do, and now she got angry all over again. They couldn't let this creep get away!

She poked the bag next to her. It was Christie. She lifted her bag and pulled at Maggie's. The three put their heads close together.

"Any ideas?" Vicky said softly.

"Sort of," Christie said. "One of us has to get out of here and get help. But how? We can't jump at this speed." She judged the truck was maintaining something like seventy miles per hour—fast, but not so fast as to get caught by a speed trap.

"Remember that Blair said one of the men was from New York? I'm sure it's this guy. He took the money. I bet that's where he's headed, and he'll have to stop for gas, unless he had a full tank. Even so . . ." Maggie's voice trailed off.

"Okay," Vicky said, "pray he stops for gas. Then one of us slips out the back, memorizes the license plate number, and calls the police from wherever we are."

"Exactly." Christie was sure they'd be able to come

up with something, and they had. "It should be Maggie, because she has the best memory."

Maggie wrinkled her forehead. She did have a good memory—for lists of Latin words and favorite poems. She'd just have to pretend the license plate was something like that.

"Maybe two of us should go," Vicky suggested, then took it back immediately. "No, too dangerous leaving one of us here alone."

The others nodded, not wanting to give voice to their thoughts. If the man discovered his extra cargo before the police could get to him, he might not think too hard about getting rid of one rice sack, but two?

Vicky's mother sat as still as one of the carved jade figurines that she collected. Ever since she had heard that her daughter was missing, she had not said a word and had barely moved a muscle, only what had been necessary to get to the police station and back. They were all sitting at one of the big round tables at The Ginger Jar. It was covered with a bright red cloth for the New Year's banquet—a banquet that had been abruptly called off. Mr. Lee had brought tea and offered food, but no one was hungry. The boys from Mansfield Hill had stayed in Chinatown, intent on searching for the girls. Teddy was with them. Old Mrs. Lee was talking quietly with Mrs. Chan, or rather Mrs. Chan was talking and Vicky's grandmother was listening, nodding every once in awhile, patting the woman's hand occasionally. Blair was taking care of Mason.

"The Porters should be here soon," Calvin Mont-gomery said. "They were going to get a plane from Bar Harbor and a cab from Logan." He was finding the wait interminable. He was used to being in con-trol of situations. He hadn't been able to control his wife's illness, and now his daughter was gone. Fear took hold and he stood up, moving to the door to watch for Maggie's parents. Gone—she couldn't be gone. He pushed the panic down. Gone—dear God, please not both of them.

An hour later, the truck made a wide turn, then an-other, and stopped. The girls sat up quickly. Maggie took off the sacks and crept to the door. They heard the man say something, but not the sound of a door closing. He wasn't pumping his own gas—probably didn't want to leave the money unattended and maybe felt a little funny about walking around car-rying a girl's shiny red knapsack decorated with a kitty face.

Maggie's stomach was upset. She didn't feel exactly sick, just very, very nervous. The other two hadn't budged. She'd patted their sacks as she moved past them and got what she assumed was a nod of encour-agement from each.

She had to go now. It wouldn't take long to fill up and pay. She opened the door cautiously and peeked out. It was a convenience store, named Christy's, ironically, and there were two lines of pumps. He'd pulled up behind another car. There was no one to the rear. She pushed the door wider and slid out. She closed it immediately and walked to the other pumps, where, as luck would have it, a family was putting gas into their Explorer, their kids racing around after what had obviously been a long time in the car. Maggie blended right in—or so she hoped.

She watched the attendant return and replace the truck's gas cap, then walk to the window on the driver's side for the money. Maggie stared at the license plate, burning the letters and numbers into her brain. New York plates. The Statue of Liberty in red in the middle of OEZ and L50. OEZ was easy and she concentrated on the others, L and 50. Her aunt Laura was turning fifty—and not overly pleased. Okay, she had it. "Oh, let it be easy for Laura at fifty." She often used tricks like this—her Latin teacher said they were called "mnemonics"—to help remember things.

Maggie itched to run inside the store, write down the numbers and letters on the plate, and call the police, but she was afraid the driver might spot her. She knew he would probably assume she was with the other family, yet there was the possibility that he might have noticed her on the street corner in Chinatown and wonder what she was doing here— which was where, by the way?

After what seemed like forever, the dark blue truck took off. She watched it go with fear—Christie and Vicky were still in the back!

Then Maggie Porter raced into the store, asked for a pen, wrote "OEZ-L50" on her palm, located the phone, picked up the receiver, and firmly pushed 911.

                    *   *   *

The Porters had arrived at The Ginger Jar and joined
the group sitting in silence around the New Year's
banquet table. After the first questions had been answered with as much information as the others had,
Maggie's parents sat sipping tea, their hands tightly
clenched together beneath the cloth. Mr. Montgomery
had stopped pacing and he, too, was sipping tea. The
phone rang and the entire table lunged after Mr. Lee,
stationed next to it, picking it up on the first ring.

"Yes, yes, where? Western Connecticut! Yes, I'll tell
them. Thank you. Do you want us to come to the
station? All right. Thank you." His voice was nervous
and tense. He turned toward the group. "A police station in western Connecticut, near Waterbury, just re-
ceived a 911 call from a Maggie Porter. She gave
them a description of a truck and its license plate
and said her friends and the money are in it. The
Connecticut police are on their way to get Maggie and
have put out an all-points bulletin on the truck in
Connecticut and New York State. The truck has New
York plates and is being driven by a young Asian
man. Detective Woo says we should remain here and
the moment he hears more, he will call us."

The Porters collapsed into each other's arms and
moved away from the group. Maggie was safe! But
Mr. Montgomery's face had turned ashen. It was
what they had feared. The girls had tried to hold on
to the money, and now Christie and Vicky were with
the thief. Had he discovered them? Were they being
held hostage and somehow Maggie had escaped? He

didn't even want to think what might happen when the police tried to stop the truck.

Mr. Lee tried to put his arm around his wife's shoulders. "It will be all right. The Year of the Dragon. It's started. Please . . ." Mrs. Lee shrugged him away and walked out of the room. Her mother-in-law followed her, but she waved her back, too.

After Maggie left, Vicky and Christie lay as still as the mice who often tried to feast on the rice in the sacks. They listened, trying to hear whether Maggie had been caught. There was no noise from the front of the truck. He hadn't even played the radio the whole trip. Maybe it didn't work. At last, they heard him start the engine. This time, it caught right away and he pulled out of the gas station and headed toward the highway. They were surprised when the truck slowed down again and turned, then came to a stop. A voice crackled over a speaker and both girls heard part of his answer: "Big Mac." Vicky could barely keep from laughing. Then when the food did come and the aroma drifted back, she had to work hard to stifle her hunger pangs. By this time, they should have been sitting down to their New Year's banquet. She thought longingly of each of the ten courses, dishes specific for the New Year and good luck. Well, she needed good luck now more than food—although the fries did smell awfully tasty.

Christie wasn't thinking of food. She was thinking of Maggie, hoping she'd been able to see the plate. What if he'd rubbed dirt on it to obscure it? If this was a stolen vehicle, that was what he'd do. At least that was what the bad guys did in the books she'd read. What if the police thought Maggie was just a little girl with an overactive imagination? But they'd at least call Boston and Detective Woo would set them straight. Still, it would all take time, and suddenly Christie began to worry that time was running out. The man had come up from New York's Chinatown—what if he made it back there with his extra produce intact? They'd have to try to escape; they'd have to . . .

The brakes squealed and the two girls clutched at each other through the coarse cloth. The truck was going off the road! Christie shoved her feet against a crate and braced her shoulders. She hoped Vicky was doing the same.

The truck came to a stop. They hadn't heard any sirens. They hadn't heard anything. Now they heard footsteps.

The door was flung open and a voice said, "All of you! Come out slowly with your hands up!"

Chapter Ten

The sight that greeted the girls caused Christie to burst into tears of relief and Vicky to start yelling, "Why didn't you say you were the police! You scared us half to death!"

The two officers with guns drawn looked slightly confused. They had been told to stop and search the truck. As the message was transmitted from unit to unit, some of the details had been omitted.

One thing was clear, however. The driver had tried to escape with a bright red bag, drawn a large knife, and was now spread-eagle against a police car, being read his rights. It was hard to imagine he could hear over the noise of his own protest, sometimes in Chinese and sometimes in English, most of it bleepable. When he saw the two girls come from the back of the truck, shocked, he stopped the steam of expletives for thirty seconds and then increased the volume.

"That's the man who stole the Chans' money!" Christie said. "He's probably got lots of illegal things in the truck, too—if it even is his truck!"

"Thank you for the help, ladies." A state police officer approached, "However, I think we'd better get you back to the station. Your friend is waiting there; then, as I understand it, half of Boston wants to see you as soon as possible."

The girls looked at each other. Surely they weren't in trouble for this?

The officer looked at them sternly. "Everything turned out all right, but you took a big chance, and if you were my kids, I'd have something to say about that." He did smile, yet Christie and Vicky could well imagine what those words might be.

Maggie was finishing a sandwich that one of the detectives at the station had gotten from a machine in the hall for her. The bread was kind of crusty and the ham very chewy, but it tasted great. When she saw her friends, she jumped up and threw her arms around them.

"What happened? Are you okay? Did he try to get away?"

"He didn't get far. Which reminds me." Christie turned to the policewoman who had driven them back. "Why didn't you guys use your sirens? Then we would have known help was on the way." She was reliving the scared feelings she'd had after Maggie left.

Before the young woman had a chance to answer, Maggie interrupted. "Sirens! Then there would have been a chase and that rickety truck could have crashed and you might have been hurt!"

The officer nodded her head. "We didn't want him to panic. We knew there were other people in the truck, but we didn't know exactly who or how many. We didn't want to take any risks."

"Good thing for me Christie was there, or you would have thought I was with him," Vicky said as the thought struck her suddenly.

The policewoman flushed. "I hope we've moved beyond making false assumptions on the basis of race. Anyway, the state police arrived just after we did and filled us in, so we knew you two weren't dangerous criminals."

Vicky finished the sentence silently: Like the driver of the truck. She really wanted to go home, but she was also somewhat apprehensive. What would her mother say?

The Connecticut State Police took them to the Massachusetts border, where they were met by a Massachusetts cruiser. It was dark by now and all three girls were tired—and safe.

Maggie and Christie entered the restaurant slightly ahead of Vicky. Their parents ran to greet them, smothering any words attempted in the closeness of their embraces. Vicky walked over to her mother, father, grandmother, and Teddy.

"I'm—" She was not able to say anything more before her mother rushed toward her, wrapped her arms around her daughter, put her head on Vicky's shoulder, and sobbed—sobbed loudly, uncontrollably, her chest heaving. Old Mrs. Lee started to join them, but her son put his arm out and whispered, "Wait!"

Vicky was stunned. She had never seen her mother

cry. Her throat closed up and her eyes stung; then she began to cry, too, saying in Chinese over and over, "I'm sorry." Still her mother did not stop, and Vicky knew instinctively that they had to be by themselves. She pulled her into one of the small rooms used for private gatherings and her mother collapsed in a large chair with arms, drawing Vicky on her lap as if she were still a small child. She stroked her daughter's hair, her face. Finally, words came. "I thought I would never see you again. I thought you were gone. It was my punishment."

"Punishment? What punishment? You have never done anything wrong. You're the best mother in the world, and you don't deserve to have a foolish daughter like me!" Vicky was astonished. What was her mother talking about?

"As you got older, I began to worry. Worry, worry all the time that something would happen to you. Just like my family. A curse. Everyone but me, gone. I thought it would happen again. Maybe if I pretended that I did not care so much, the luck would be good." Mrs. Lee broke down again.

And there it was, the answer that had been staring Vicky in the face these last years, only she hadn't been able to see it. Irrationally, her mother had been afraid of getting too attached to her own daughter for fear of bringing bad luck, attracting evil spirits— spirits that had caused Mrs. Lee to lose her own mother, father, sister, cousins. If you built a wall between yourself and someone you loved, maybe the wall would keep that person safe.

"Oh Mom," Vicky said, kissing her mother softly on the cheek. "You're not going to lose me." As she said it, though, she thought that it might have come true. In trying to avoid bad luck and keeping her daughter at a distance, Mrs. Lee over the years would have lost Vicky, and neither would have known why.

Mr. Lee slipped into the room. His wife and daughter turned to him, radiant smiles on both their faces. Immediately, his wife said to him, "How can I go back and face those people? I am so embarrassed!" She put her hands to her face and tried to wipe it dry. She tried to pat her hair into place.

"No one has noticed anything. They are much too busy with their own reunions, and I want mine!"

Vicky flew into her father's arms. "Don't be mad at me—or Teddy. We made him do it. We couldn't let the Chans lose their money or Blair her education!"

"Your heart is in the right place, my daughter, but sometimes your thoughts are not. And Teddy and I have already had our talk. Now, come and eat. Aren't you hungry?"

It was her father's universal cure and Vicky laughed. "Not the New Year's banquet this late!" Much as she had been dreaming of it, she really wasn't in the mood.

"No, we will do that tomorrow night. But I am sure you will not refuse some pot stickers now."

Vicky wasn't about to say no. She took her mother's hand, and after they had both washed their faces and combed their hair in the ladies' room, mother watched daughter consume a mountain of succulent pot stickers. Now that the long wait was over, they were slightly giddy with relief—and hungry.

It wasn't an ordinary Monday at school. Mark and Scott had spread the word from Mansfield Hill all over Cabot. Blair, Vicky, Christie, and Maggie were greeted with "Way to go!" as well as the Cabot cheer when they returned to campus in the morning in time for their first class. Even their meeting with Mrs. Babcox, who had been following events by phone all day Sunday, hadn't been as bad as the girls, especially Blair, had feared. Blair told Mrs. Babcox, "I know I should have explained to you what was going on, but I could not convince my mother that you might be able to help. And I could not disobey her. I will understand why you cannot have a girl like me here." She hung her head. Maggie started to protest, but Christie stopped her. And then Mrs. Babcox spoke.

"It is very frightening to be in a country where you do not speak the language or know anyone," said the headmistress. "The only people to blame in all this are the men who tried to take advantage of your family and who have done it to others. I know you were trying to do what was best, and that is exactly the kind of girl we want at Cabot. And I know Blair Samuels will be proud of you. We must both write to her soon."

Blair's smile returned.

"However, you three took a chance that might have had disastrous consequences." Mrs. Babcox sighed. It was hard to be angry with these three eighth-graders, who had also done what they thought was right. "Please, promise me you won't do anything like this again. I don't think my nerves can take it."

It was an easy promise to make, especially if you had your fingers crossed behind your back, as Christie & Company did.

They left, having been given permission to return to The Ginger Jar that evening for the postponed celebration of the Year of the Dragon. The Porters were staying in town another day and Calvin Montgomery would join them at the restaurant, as well as the Chans. Mark Reese and Scott Franklin had also been invited. The Lees were very grateful for the boys' help. They had not stopped searching until they heard the girls were safe. Vicky saw red envelopes in their future.

When they left the headmistress's office to go to class, Blair told them, "It is not true any longer that my mother doesn't have friends here. Your father"—she nodded at Christie—"is going to help her with all her legal work. One of the partners in his firm speaks Chinese. And you have already heard what your parents are doing!" she said to Vicky.

Vicky nodded. When she had told her mother about the Chans' apartment, Mrs. Lee had refused to let them return there even for one night. The Lees were very active in the Asian community and this morning Mrs. Lee was taking Mrs. Chan to see about a reasonable apartment in Brookline where there would be others who spoke Chinese, day care for Mason, and a job as a seamstress at a friend's shop. "She is always looking for good workers," Mrs. Lee told her daughter. Vicky was proud of the way her mother had so efficiently solved most of Mrs. Chan's problems. But what was staying with her and giving the day a particularly warm glow, despite the falling temperature and prediction of a big storm, was the memory of her mother's kiss good-bye, a kiss freely offered and heartily returned.

"Maggie and her friends think they're such a big deal. It makes me want to puke." A familiar voice rang out from the classroom Maggie was just about to enter. It was Amber St. James.

Maggie stood for a moment and decided to wait for some other students to come. It would feel distinctly awkward to walk in now. Amber would be sure to realize that Maggie had heard what she had just said, and kept on saying.

"Our precious little poet. It was fun to string her along for a while. She never realized we were doing a number on her. Imagine a bumpkin from Maine thinking she can write. I mean, duh!"

Whomever she was talking to was quick to agree. One of Amber's new followers? "Really, I don't believe a word of it. It's ridiculous to think they saved that Chinese girl's money and captured some guy who's on the Most Wanted list."

"Little Margaret is prone to exaggeration, and I'm sure this is no exception." Amber laughed. "You should have seen her face after I cut her hair. It was a scream! I wish I had a video."

Maggie was beginning to boil over. She started to charge into the room, words frothing from her mouth, but a third voice stopped her. Someone seated farther away from the door.

"Oh it's all true, Miss St. James. And don't you wish it wasn't? As for Maggie's hair, I wouldn't brag about that little trick if I were you. Besides, she ended up even better than ever. You should look so good—in your dreams."

It was Priscilla, another member of the writing seminar and also a tenth grader. Maggie had liked her immediately and thought her work was wonderful.

Now she really couldn't go in. Where was everybody else? Where was Mr. Ropeik?

While she was waiting, she thought about what a jerk she had been. How could she not have known what Amber was doing? But she had never met anyone like her before. Friends didn't do stuff like that to other friends, and she had thought Amber was her friend. Friends! She'd been a real jerk with them, too. She was remembering her trip to Harvard Square. As soon as she saw them, she'd tell them. The thought made her feel a whole lot better. A good start for the New Year!

The rest of the class and the teacher arrived all at once and swept Maggie into the room with them. Mr. Ropeik had heard something about Christie & Company's adventure.

"Maggie, you seem to be choosing some pretty drastic ways to gather material! I want you to write it all up for us. Use the form that seems best—poetry, narrative—let it flow. And judging from what we've seen from you so far, it should be great."

She knew it was childish, immature, beneath her, but Maggie didn't care. She turned around toward Amber, who was slumped in the corner, twirling an earring in what looked like an infected hole, stared at her former idol hard, and stuck out her tongue.

Then she turned back and concentrated on the poem by Yeats that Mr. Ropeik was reading. " 'I will arise and go now, and go to Innisfree . . .' " She closed her eyes—and was there.

Chapter Eleven

Teddy had gone to Aleford to get Christie & Company and the boys from Mansfield Hill. "This time, you've outdone yourself, cousin," he told her. "I have a story good enough for the front page of the *Harvard Crimson!*"

"I hope the snow holds off," said Maggie peering out the window. The sky had been threatening all day.

"I hope it doesn't," said Christie. "Think how much fun it would be to get snowbound at The Ginger Jar."

When Maggie walked into the restaurant, which was filled with fragrant bowls of narcissus and vases of plum blossoms mixed with the even more enticing aromas coming from the kitchen, she agreed. Everything looked so beautiful. Besides the tables with their red cloths, long strips of red paper covered with poems in Chinese, messages of good fortune, and pictures of dragons decorated the walls and doorways. The Lees came to greet them, their faces red, too, flushed from the steamy kitchen.

"Give me your coats," Mr. Lee ordered, "and have some tea to warm up. The others will be here soon and we can begin!"

When Vicky took off her coat and hat, her mother looked at her in surprise. "Why are you dressed like this?" she asked, staring hard at Vicky's navy slacks, demure white blouse, and navy sweater worn buttoned up to her collar. Her hair was in one long braid.

"I thought you would like it," Vicky protested.

Old Mrs. Lee started to laugh. "You two need to get your signals straight! I learned this phrase from one of my friends. It means—"

"We know what it means," Vicky said, taking her sweater off. "And you're right! I'll be back. I want to comb my hair!"

"I guess I was more used to our peacock than a guinea hen," Mrs. Lee said ruefully to her mother-in-law. "But I still don't like all those smells!" She wrinkled up her nose.

Soon everyone had taken their places at the tables and the banquet began—that is, everyone except Mr. and Mrs. Lee. "It is the Chinese custom for us to serve you. Please, eat! We will join you later."

Vicky and her friends had a table to themselves, and when the first course arrived, everyone looked to her for an explanation.

"You have to pace yourself. A Chinese banquet is a little like a marathon. We'll have ten courses, because ten is a lucky number. So is the number eight. It means you're going to be rich or get something valuable. Four is a very bad number. It means death. When my parents opened the restaurant, they were issued a number for collecting sales tax. It was filled with fours! My mother called the tax department and told them, 'I can't have this number! It means my business will fail and I won't be able to pay you any taxes!' They probably thought she was crazy, but they did give her a new number."

"Everything in Chinese means something," Maggie mused. "It gives you so much to think about."

"I'm thinking about what I'm eating right now, and it's delicious—whatever it is," Mark said.

Blair enlightened him. "Many New Year's banquets start with this plate of cold appetizers and the one you just ate was jellyfish!"

"Jellyfish!" Christie thought they were getting awfully close to chicken-feet territory.

"Try it," Mark urged. "I'm going to eat everything."

To reassure her guests, Vicky pointed out the rest of the items on the plate. "We always have five things. This is shrimp, that's chicken, and those thin slices of meat are Five-Spiced Beef. What looks like a flower in the middle is a hard-cooked egg, and the jellyfish you know."

"The food has to be as beautiful to the eye as it is to the stomach," Blair told them. She had not seen or eaten food like this since she arrived in the United States. She looked over at her mother, who was talking to some people at another table. Mason was in his stroller at her side, happily batting at the big round beads strung across it. He was wearing his best clothes, his tiger clothes, given to him at birth. His feet were covered with silk slippers with tigers embroidered on them and he wore a similar hat. His bib had a tiger, too. In China, the tiger is the king of beasts and protects children.

Mr. Lee was making an announcement. "Normally, we have the soup at the end of the meal, but because so many of you here are used to eating it near the beginning, we'll have it now." He repeated the explanation in Chinese and tureens of fragrant shark's fin soup were placed on the tables.

Each course that followed seemed more special than the one before. The Porters and Mr. Montgomery were loud in their praises.

"I haven't had food like this outside of Beijing," Mr. Montgomery told the Lees, who beamed with pleasure. His work had often taken him to Asia.

"Listen." Christie lowered her voice. "My father is going to start talking about how the Chinese were the first to invent everything. He's always coming home with something else one of his law partners, Susan Chen, has added to the list."

"Usually, it's my father who says this," Vicky told them, "but outside the family, he would consider it bragging."

"The compass, clocks, paper, movable type, silk, of course, gunpowder. Let's see, what else?" Mr. Montgomery was reciting his list.

Mr. Lee couldn't resist after all. "Spaghetti, fireworks, orange trees, acupuncture, porcelain, and paddleboats, plus some others I have forgotten."

The adults turned in surprise as the kids all burst into laughter. But before someone could ask what the joke was, more food diverted everyone's attention.

There were Goldfish Shrimp that looked like real shrimp swimming on the plate—jumbo shrimp assembled with bits of smaller shrimp, green peas for eyes, and a tiny bit of ham for a mouth; large mushrooms stuffed with spicy ground pork and decorated with thin slices of vegetables cut to look like flowers and leaves; Sesame Chicken—a large, thin piece of white meat rolled around black mushrooms, green vegetables, and red Chinese ham before being rolled up, sliced thin, and coated with the seeds and cooked, the pretty spiral crispy on the outside; then Tea-Smoked Duck, surrounded by steamed buns to hold the succulent meat.

"I see why you said it's like a marathon," said Scott, "but I'm still going strong. What's next?"

"You have to have fish on New Year's. This preparation is very pretty. The outside of the fish is scored—you know, crosshatched—then deep-fried. See?" She pointed to the dish set on the table before them. "The fish stands up on its mouth and all the meat falls in a pattern around the sauce. The sauce is red—"

"We know—for good luck," Christie said good-naturedly.

"I feel like we are teaching you a course in Chinese customs," Blair said. "We have to have fish at New Year's, and we also have to have some left over, because the Chinese word for fish—*yu*—sounds like the one meaning 'plenty.' If we were having this meal on the actual New Year's Eve, it would mean we'd have something to eat in the New Year, the next day."

"I love this course," Maggie said. She was taking mental notes and already planning to write about the experience in her journal. She knew that she was sharing a very special event, not just the celebration of a new beginning of the year but also a new beginning for the Chans.

A platter of vegetables arrived, the tender part of the pea pod, then a noodle dish—long noodles for a long life.

The meal ended with Eight Treasure Rice. "This is not really so hard to make," Vicky told them. "It's fun to do. You put some sweet rice in a bowl, then add a layer of seven fruits, things like dates and raisins, with a red bean in the middle, then more rice on top, and you turn the bowl over. It's like a mold. See the design of the fruits?"

"You only said seven. What's the eighth treasure?" Christie asked.

"The rice!" Blair answered for Vicky. "It's our most valuable treasure!"

The tables were filled with dishes, yet no one was in a hurry to get up. More jasmine tea arrived and everyone lingered, talking, telling stories.

Christie was trying to teach Scott how to use chopsticks to pick up the last of the "treasures." He told her he could eat more with a fork but that he'd give it a shot. Such a well-coordinated diver, yet he couldn't seem to make his fingers work together!

Vicky went over to thank her parents. "This is the happiest New Year I've ever had."

"Certainly the most unusual," her father replied,

thinking back to the day before. "But yes, the happiest."

Mrs. Lee just smiled.

Scott and Christie were still fooling around with the chopsticks. Mark had asked Vicky to translate some of the poems that decorated the room. As they got up, he suddenly remembered something. "Hey, you never told me my sign."

"The rooster!" Vicky said.

"Oh, I wanted it to be the dragon." He sounded slightly disappointed.

"The rooster is a very, very good sign. It means you have lots of self-confidence and are a perfectionist, but with the ability to get things done. Roosters like to travel."

"Maybe to China." Mark seemed pleased now.

Maggie and Blair got up to join their parents. As she pushed her chair back, Maggie wondered if she'd ever have a Mark or a Scott. Not that her friends were going steady, but these boys were definitely interested in them. Perhaps she'd end up devoting her life to her art. It sounded noble, except she wasn't sure how it would be in real life. But maybe there was someone out there.

"What is this place? It's like something from one of the history books!" A young man dressed in silver stepped from a jet-propelled craft and approached the house that seemed to date from the nineteenth century, eons ago. His companion cautioned him. "It appears

to be covered in some sort of vegetation. I don't think we should proceed."

"Maybe not, but I can't leave this place without a look. Something seems to be pulling me inside."

"It could be a variant ray. Or if not, alien gases may be trapped in the structure. We must get back to the ship."

"You leave if you want," he answered defiantly. "I'm going in!"

With that, he mounted the stairs, the old wood giving way at the top. He jumped to one side and avoided getting stuck. He quickly cut through the vines with his laser and the front door swung open. The place was deserted, though filled with many quaint artifacts that he would return and catalog. He recognized a television set from sometime in the late twentieth century. And everything undisturbed. What a find! He slowly ascended a stairway to a balcony that surrounded the room below. Then he saw her.

The woman was dressed in a long white gown, her long hair softly waving to her waist. She was lying on something he believed they had called "a couch." A book—he had seen books in the museum—was open at her side.

What apparition was this? What sort of creature? She looked human, yet did not move. Her eyes were closed. Again he felt as if some invisible thread was drawing him insistently forward, and he found himself at her side, gazing down into her lovely face. Without thinking, he kissed her soft lips.

Slowly, her eyes opened. She . . .

"Maggie! Wake up!" Vicky said. She and Christie were at Maggie's side. Her chair hadn't budged. "Your dad wants to take a picture of us three. He says he's going to call it 'Christie and Company in the Year of the Dragon!'"

Long-Life Noodles

Serves four

6 cups chicken broth, homemade or canned
3 tablespoons cornstarch
1 cup cooked chicken, cut into 1-inch squares
20 small shrimp, fresh or frozen, without shells
½–¾ cup snow peas
3 tablespoons soy sauce
2 teaspoons salt (optional)
2 eggs, beaten
½ tablespoon sesame oil
1 pound fresh or dried Chinese noodles (lo mein, for
  example)

In a large pot, start to bring the water for the noodles
to a boil. Meanwhile, boil the chicken broth in another pot. When the broth comes to a boil, sprinkle
the cornstarch on top and whisk it into the liquid
until dissolved. Reduce the heat and add the chicken,
shrimp, and snow peas. Season with the soy sauce

and salt (if desired). You won't need the salt if your broth already has salt in it. Add the beaten eggs and stir carefully. When the mixture is heated through, turn off the heat and splash the sesame oil on top.

Once the water in the other pot has come to a boil, cook the noodles according to the directions on the package or from the store. Drain and divide the noodles among four bowls. Pour equal amounts of the soup over each and serve. If you can find Chinese soup spoons, use these with chopsticks and enjoy a long life!

This dish is traditionally served at birthdays and during the Chinese New Year. The long noodles symbolize longevity. All the ingredients are available in Asian markets and in some supermarkets and health-food stores. The soup will taste just as good and will be just as lucky if you substitute a pound of dried Italian pasta, such as cappellini (angel hair pasta), and thinly sliced cucumber or another green vegetable for the snow peas.

*   *   *

My thanks to Kathy and Jasmine Chang for helping me with information about all the food and Chinese customs, especially this recipe.

The Chinese use a lunar calendar, one based on the phases of the moon. The new moon marks the beginning of each month and the full moon signals the middle of the month. On the calendar that we use in the Western world, the Chinese New Year always falls sometime between January 21 and February 20.

The Western zodiac is divided into twelve months, each with a celestial sign. The Chinese zodiac is based on a twelve-year cycle. Each year is represented by an animal sign. Look at the chart above to find your sign. Maggie, Christie, and Vicky were all born in 1983, the Year of the Pig, or Boar.

Over the centuries, the Chinese have placed a great deal of importance on a person's sign, believing that it can determine one's character and destiny. For example, those born in the Year of the Dragon will be lucky and strong; those whose sign is the Dog, loyal and dependable. The Pig stands for wealth, honesty, the ability to make many friends, stubbornness, and accomplishing what one sets out to do. Does this sound like Christie & Company?

144